'My God!
A whole minute
of bliss! Is that
really so little
for the whole of
a man's life?'

FYODOR DOSTOYEVSKY
Born 1821, Moscow, Russia
Died 1881, Saint Petersburg, Russia

'White Nights' was first published in its original Russian as *Belye Nochi* in 1848. 'Bobok' first appeared in 1873; the title means 'little bean.' Both are taken from the *The Gambler and Other Stories*, translated by Ronald Meyer.

DOSTOYEVSKY IN PENGUIN CLASSICS

Crime and Punishment
The Idiot
Demons
The Double
The Gambler and Other Stories
The Grand Inquisitor
Notes from the Underground
Netochka Nezvanova
The House of the Dead
The Brothers Karamazov
The Village of Stepanchikovo
Russian Short Stories from Pushkin to Buida

FYODOR DOSTOYEVSKY

White Nights

Translated by
Ronald Meyer

PENGUIN BOOKS

PENGUIN CLASSICS

UK | USA | Canada | Ireland | Australia
India | New Zealand | South Africa

Penguin Classics is part of the Penguin Random House group
of companies whose addresses can be found at global.
penguinrandomhouse.com.

Penguin Random House UK
One Embassy Gardens, 8 Viaduct Gardens, London SW11 7BW

penguin.co.uk

Penguin
Random House
UK

This edition published in Penguin Classics 2016

036

Set in 9.5/13 pt Baskerville 10 Pro
Typeset by Jouve (UK), Milton Keynes
Printed and bound in Great Britain by Clays Ltd, Elcograf S.p.A.

The authorized representative in the EEA is Penguin Random House
Ireland, Morrison Chambers, 32 Nassau Street, Dublin D02 YH68

A CIP catalogue record for this book is available from the British Library

ISBN: 978-0-241-25208-6

Contents

White Nights

A SENTIMENTAL LOVE STORY
(FROM THE MEMOIRS OF A DREAMER)

> . . . Or was his destiny from the start
> To be but just one moment
> Near your heart? . . .
>
> – Ivan Turgenev

THE FIRST NIGHT

It was a wonderful night, the kind of night, dear reader, which is only possible when we are young. The sky was so starry, it was such a bright sky that looking at it you could not help but ask yourself: is it really possible for bad-tempered and capricious people to live under such a sky? That is also a young person's question, dear reader, a very young person's question, but may the Lord ask it of your heart more often! . . . Speaking of capricious and sundry bad-tempered gentlemen, I could not help but recall my own commendable conduct throughout the whole day. From early morning an astonishing

1

melancholy had started to torment me. It suddenly seemed that I, so alone, was being abandoned by everyone – that everyone was deserting me. Well, of course, anyone is entitled to ask: who is 'everyone'? Because I've been living in Petersburg eight years now and I've hardly been able to make a single acquaintance. But what do I need acquaintances for? I'm acquainted with all of Petersburg as it is; that's why it seemed to me that everyone was abandoning me when all of Petersburg suddenly up and left for their dachas. I was terrified of being left alone, and for three whole days I wandered about the city in a state of deep melancholy, not understanding in the least what was happening to me. No matter whether I went to Nevsky Prospekt, or the park, or wandered along the embankment – there wasn't a single person of those whom I have been accustomed to meet for a year now in the same place, at a certain time. Of course, they don't know me, but I know them. I know them intimately; I have practically learned their faces by heart – and I admire them when they are cheerful, and I'm crestfallen when they grow sad. I almost struck up a friendship with a certain little old man, whom I meet every blessed day, at a certain hour on the Fontanka. His face is so dignified and thoughtful; he's always whispering under his breath and gesticulating with his left hand, while in his right hand he holds a long gnarled walking-stick with a golden knob. He's even noticed me and shows a cordial concern for me. Should it happen that I'm not at the same place on the Fontanka at a certain hour, I'm positive that he would be crestfallen. That's why we sometimes almost greet each other, particularly when we're both in a good mood. The other day, when we had not seen each other for two whole days and met on the third day, we almost reached for our hats, but, thank goodness, we came to our senses in time, lowered our hands and passed each other by in sympathy. I also have houses that are my acquaintances. As I walk, it's as if each one I come to runs out into the street in front of me, looks out at me with its windows wide open and almost says: 'Hello, how do you do? And I, thank God, am well, but in May they're going to add a floor to me.' Or: 'How do you do? And I'm having some repairs done tomorrow.' Or: 'I almost burned down and I was so scared', and so forth. I have favourites among them, some are intimate friends; one of them intends to be treated by an architect this summer. I'll make it a point to drop by every day so that, God forbid, they don't kill it in the process! . . . But I will never forget what happened to a certain very pretty, light-pink little house. It was such a sweet little stone house; it looked at me so cordially, and so haughtily at its ungainly neighbours, that my heart would rejoice when I chanced to walk past. Suddenly, last week, I was walking down the street and upon turning to look at my friend – I heard a plaintive cry: 'But they're going to paint me yellow!' The scoundrels! Barbarians! They spared nothing: neither the columns, nor

3

the cornices, and my friend had turned as yellow as a canary. I almost had an attack of jaundice myself, and to this day I do not have the strength to see my poor disfigured friend who was painted the colour of the Celestial Empire.

So now you understand, reader, how I am acquainted with all of Petersburg.

I have already said that for three whole days I was tormented with anxiety until I guessed the reason for it. And on the street I was in a bad way (this one's gone, that one's gone, where's so-and-so got to?) – and I wasn't myself at home either. For two evenings I tried to put a finger on what it was I found wanting in my room. Why was I so uncomfortable staying there? And with bewilderment I examined my green, sooty walls, and the ceiling from which hung a cobweb that Matryona had been cultivating with such resounding success; I looked over all my furniture, examined every chair, wondering if that was the problem (because I'm not myself if even one chair isn't in the same place as it was the day before); I looked out the window, but it was all in vain . . . I didn't feel any better. I even took it into my head to summon Matryona and give her there and then a fatherly reprimand for the cobweb and for her slovenliness in general; but she merely looked at me in amazement and walked away without a word in response, so that the cobweb hangs there safe and sound to this day. It was only this morning that I finally guessed what the matter was! Oh! Why, they're all making off to their dachas and leaving me behind! Forgive the trivial style, but I'm not up to lofty turns of speech . . . because, you see, everybody in Petersburg had either moved or is moving to their dacha; because after hiring a cab, every venerable gentleman of a solid appearance was immediately transformed before my eyes into a venerable father of a family, who after his daily official duties sets off without luggage to the bosom of his family, at the dacha; because every passer-by now has a quite special air about him, which all but says to every person he meets: 'Gentlemen, I'm only here in passing, but in two hours I'm leaving for my dacha.' If a window opens, upon which slender fingers as white as sugar had just drummed, and out leans the head of a pretty girl, who calls to a pedlar with jugs of flowers – I immediately, there and then, imagine that these flowers are being bought not simply so as to take pleasure in the spring and flowers in a stuffy city apartment, but because everybody is moving to their dacha and they'll be taking the flowers with them. Moreover, I had already made such strides in my new, special sort of discovery that I could already unerringly identify on the basis of appearance alone where their dacha was located. The residents of Kamenny and Aptekarsky islands or the Peterhof Road were distinguished by the studied elegance of their movements, their foppish summer suits and the handsome carriages that brought them to the city. The inhabitants of Pargolovo and further out at first glance 'inspired' one with their prudence and respectability; the visitor to Krestovsky Island was distinguished by his unruffled, cheerful air. Whether I managed to run into a long procession of carters holding the reins as they lazily walked alongside their carts, loaded with whole mountains of furniture of every description – tables, chairs, couches both Turkish and non-Turkish – and other household goods and chattels, on which, on top of everything, frequently would be sitting at the very summit of the load, the wizened cook, keeping watch over her master's goods as the apple of her eye; whether I looked at the boats, heavily laden with household utensils, as they glided down the Neva or Fontanka to Chernaya River or the islands – the carts and boats increased tenfold, a hundredfold before my very eyes, it seemed as though everything had up and left, that whole caravans had moved to the dacha; it seemed that all of Petersburg threatened to turn into a desert, so that in the end I became ashamed, hurt and sad: I had absolutely nowhere to go and no reason to go to a dacha. I was ready to leave with every cart, to drive off with every gentleman of venerable appearance who was hiring a cabbie, but no one, absolutely no one invited me; it was as if I indeed was a stranger to them!

I had been walking a lot and for a long time, and I had already completely succeeded, as was my wont, in forgetting where I was, when I suddenly found myself at the city gates. I cheered up in an instant, and stepped to the other side of the barrier, walked between the sown fields and the meadows, oblivious of any fatigue, but sensing with all my being that some burden was being lifted from my soul. All the passers-by looked at me so cordially that we practically bowed to one another; everybody was so happy about something, every last one was smoking a cigar. And I was happy as I had never been before. It was as if I had suddenly found myself in Italy – nature had so strongly affected me, a semi-invalid city dweller who had almost died of suffocation within the city's walls.

There is something inexplicably touching in our Petersburg nature, when with the advent of spring she suddenly displays all her might, all the powers granted her by heaven, when she bursts into leaves, dresses herself up and decks herself out in colourful flowers . . . Somehow I can't help but be reminded of that weak and sickly girl, at whom you sometimes look with pity, sometimes with a compassionate love, and sometimes you simply do not notice her, but then suddenly, for a moment, she somehow, unexpectedly, becomes inexplicably, wonderfully beautiful, and you, startled and intoxicated, unwittingly ask yourself: What power caused those sad, thoughtful eyes to shine with such fire? What summoned the blood to those pale, sunken cheeks? What has suffused those tender features of her face with passion? Why does that breast heave so? What was it that so suddenly summoned strength, life and beauty to the poor girl's face that it began to shine with such a smile, came to life with such a sparkling, effervescent laugh? You look around, you search for someone, you hazard a guess ... But the moment passes and perhaps tomorrow you will once again meet the same thoughtful and distracted gaze as before, the same pale face, the same submissive and timid movements, and even repentance, even traces of some sort of deadening melancholy and annoyance at the short-lived exhilaration ... And you regret that the momentary beauty faded so quickly, so irretrievably, that it flashed before you so deceptively and in vain – you regret this because there was not time for you even to fall in love with her ...

But nevertheless my night was better than my day! Here's what happened:

I arrived back in the city very late, and it had already struck ten o'clock as I approached my apartment. My path ran along the embankment of the canal, where at that hour you will not find a living soul. True, I live in a very remote part of the city. I was walking and singing, because when I am happy I am sure to hum something to myself, like every other happy man who has neither friends nor good acquaintances and who in a joyful moment has nobody with whom he can share his joy. Suddenly the most unexpected adventure happened to me.

Somewhat to the side, leaning against the railing of the canal, stood a woman. With her elbows resting on the railing, she seemed to be looking very attentively at the canal's turbid water. She was wearing a very pretty yellow hat and a bewitching black mantilla. 'She's a young girl, she just has to be a brunette,' I thought. It seems she had not heard my steps; she didn't even stir when I walked past, with bated breath, and with my heart beating violently. 'Strange!' I thought, 'she must be completely absorbed by something', and suddenly I stopped, rooted to the ground. I had heard a muffled sob. Yes! I hadn't been deceived: the girl was crying and a minute later there was another whimper and then another. My God! My heart sank. And no matter how great my timidness with women, this was hardly the time! . . . I turned around, took a step in her direction and would certainly have uttered the word 'Madam', but for the fact that I knew that this exclamation had already been uttered a thousand times in all our Russian society novels. That was the only thing that stopped me. But while I was searching for a word, the girl came to her senses, glanced back, recollected where she was, cast her eyes down and slipped past me along the embankment. I set off after her at once, but when she realized this, she quit the embankment, crossed the street and set out walking down the pavement. My heart was fluttering, like a captured little bird. Suddenly a certain incident came to my aid.

On the sidewalk across the street, not far from my unknown girl, there suddenly appeared a gentleman in evening dress, a man with a solid number of years behind him, but whose gait was anything but solid. He walked, reeling, and carefully leaning against the wall. The girl meanwhile walked as straight as an arrow, hurriedly and timidly, as girls generally do when they don't want someone to offer to see them home at night, and of course, the teetering gentleman would never have caught up with her if my good fortune had not given him the idea of looking to unnatural methods. Suddenly, without saying a word to anyone, my gentleman darts off and flies as fast as his legs will carry him; and running, he catches up with my unknown girl. She was moving along like the wind, but the staggering gentleman was overtaking her, he had overtaken her, the girl cried out – and . . . I thank my good fortune for my excellent knotty walking-stick, which just happened to be in my right hand on this occasion. In an instant I found myself on the sidewalk across the street; in an instant the uninvited gentleman understood what was what, took into account my incontrovertible reasoning, fell silent and dropped behind, and only when we were already quite far away did he reproach me in rather energetic terms. But his words scarcely reached us.

'Give me your hand,' I said to my unknown girl, 'and he won't dare bother us anymore.'

In silence she gave me her hand, which was still trembling from nervousness and fright. Oh, unbidden gentleman! How grateful I was to you at that moment! I cast a cursory glance at her: she was very pretty and a brunette – I had guessed right; on her black eyelashes still shone the tears of her recent fright or former sorrow – I don't know which. But on her lips a smile already sparkled. She also cast a furtive glance at me, blushed and looked down.

'Now then, you see, why did you drive me away? If I'd been there, nothing would have happened . . .'

'But I didn't know you: I thought that you too . . .'

'But do you really know me now?'

'A little bit. Now then, for example, why are you trembling?'

'Oh, you guessed right from the very first!' I answered, delighted that my girl was clever: that is never a bad thing where beauty is concerned. 'Yes, you guessed from the very first glance the sort of person you're dealing with. Yes, it's true, it's true, I'm timid with women, I'm nervous, I won't deny it – no less than you were a moment ago when that gentleman frightened you . . . I'm frightened now. It's like a dream, but even in my dreams I never guessed that I would ever talk with a woman.'

'What? Really? . . .'

'Yes, if my hand is trembling, then it's because such a pretty small hand like yours has never clasped it before. I've grown quite unused to women; that is, I never became used to them; you see, I'm alone . . . I don't even know how to talk to them. Even now I don't know whether I've said something stupid to you. Tell me frankly; I should tell you that I don't take offence easily . . .'

'No, nothing, nothing; on the contrary. And since you're already asking me to be candid, then I will tell you that women like such timidity; and if you want to know more, then I like it as well, and I won't send you away until we reach my house.'

'You'll make it so,' I began, gasping with delight, 'that at once I'll stop being my timid self, and then – farewell, all my methods! . . .'

'Methods? What sort of methods, for what? Now that's not very nice.'

'Guilty, I won't do it anymore, it was a slip of the tongue; but how do you expect me at a moment like this to have no desire . . .'

'To be liked, is that it?'

'Well, yes; yes, for God's sake, be kind. Consider who I am! You see, I'm already twenty-six years old, but I don't ever see anyone. So then, how can I speak well, cleverly and to the point? It will be to your advantage if everything comes out in the open . . . I don't know how to keep quiet when my heart is speaking inside me. Well, it doesn't matter . . . Believe it or not, not a single woman, ever, ever! No acquaintances at all! And all I dream of every day is that at long last I will finally meet someone. Oh, if only you knew how many times I've fallen in love like that! . . .'

'But how, with whom? . . .'

'Why with nobody, with an ideal, with the one I see in my dreams. I create entire love stories in my dreams. Oh, you don't know me! It's true, of course, I couldn't help meeting two or three women, but what sort of women were they? They were all landladies or something like that. But I'll make you laugh, when I tell you that several times I have thought of striking up a conversation just like that, without ceremony, with some aristocratic lady on the street, when she is alone, it goes without saying; to speak, of course, timidly, respectfully, deferentially, ardently; to say that I am perishing all alone, so that she wouldn't drive me away, that I don't have the means to get to know any woman; to suggest to her that a woman is duty-bound not to spurn the timid entreaty of such an unfortunate man as I. That in the end all that I'm asking her for is merely to say a few brotherly words to me, with sympathy, not to drive me away at the very first moment, to take me at my word, to listen to what I have to say, to laugh at me if she likes, to give me hope, to say a few words to me, just a few words, even if we never meet again afterwards! . . . You're laughing . . . But then that's why I'm telling you . . .'

'Don't be annoyed; I'm laughing at the fact that you are your own worst enemy, and if you had tried, perhaps you might have succeeded, even though it was all taking place on the street; the simpler, the better . . . Not a single kind-hearted woman, provided she wasn't silly or particularly angry about something at that moment, could have brought herself to send you away without those few words that you pleaded for so timidly . . . But what am I saying! Of course, she would have taken you for a madman. You see, I was judging by myself. But I know a lot about how people on this earth live!'

'Oh, thank you!' I cried out, 'you don't know what you've done for me today!'

'Very well, very well! But tell me, how did you recognize me to be the sort of woman, with whom . . . well, whom you considered worthy . . . of attention and friendship . . . in a word, not a landlady, as you put it. Why did you make up your mind to approach me?'

'Why? Why? But you were alone, that gentleman was too brazen, it's night now: you must agree that it was my duty . . .'

'No, no, even earlier, there, on the other side. You wanted to approach me then, didn't you?'

'There, on the other side? But I truly don't know how to answer; I'm afraid . . . Do you know, today I was happy; I was walking, singing; I'd been on the outskirts of the city; I'd never experienced such happy moments before. You . . . it seemed to me, perhaps . . . Well, forgive me for reminding you: it seemed to me that you were crying, and I . . . I couldn't bear to hear it . . . it made my heart ache . . . Oh, my God! Surely I might feel pangs of anguish for you? Surely it was not a sin to experience brotherly compassion for you! . . . Forgive me, I said compassion . . . Well, yes, in a word, could I really have offended you by impulsively taking it into my head to approach you? . . .'

'Stop, enough, don't speak . . .' the girl said, having cast her eyes downward and squeezing my hand. 'I'm the one who's guilty for bringing it up; but I'm glad that

I wasn't mistaken about you . . . But here, I'm already home; I need to go that way, down the lane, it's only a stone's throw away . . . Goodbye, thank you . . .'

'But is it possible, is it really possible that we shall never see each other again? . . . Is it possible it will end like this?'

'There, you see,' the girl said, laughing, 'at first you wanted just two words, and now . . . However, I won't say anything . . . Perhaps we'll meet . . .'

'I'll come here tomorrow,' I said. 'Oh, forgive me, I'm already making demands . . .'

'Yes, you're impatient . . . you are practically demanding . . .'

'Listen, listen!' I interrupted her. 'Forgive me if I again say something not quite . . . But here it is: I can't help coming here tomorrow. I'm a dreamer; I have so little real life that I regard such moments as this one, now, to be so rare that I can't help repeating these moments in my dreams. I will dream of you all night, for an entire week, all year long. I will come here tomorrow without fail, exactly here, to this very spot, exactly at this time, and I'll be happy as I recall what happened yesterday. This place is already dear to me. I already have two or three such places in Petersburg. Once I even shed tears, because of a memory, like you . . . Who knows, perhaps ten minutes ago you, too, were crying because of a memory . . . But forgive me, I've forgotten myself again; perhaps at one time you were particularly happy here . . .'

'Very well,' the girl said, 'perhaps I will come here tomorrow, also at ten o'clock. I see that I can't forbid you . . . The fact of the matter is that I have to be here; don't think that I'm arranging a meeting with you; I'm warning you in advance that I need to be here for myself. But, you see . . . Well, I'll tell you frankly: it would be nice if you did come; in the first place, there might be some more unpleasantness like today, but that's beside the point . . . in a word, I'd simply like to see you . . . so I could say a few words to you. Only please don't think ill of me now. Don't think that I arrange meetings so casually . . . I would have made one, if . . . But let that be my secret! Only we must make an agreement in advance . . .'

'An agreement! Speak, tell me, tell me all beforehand; I'll agree to everything, I'm ready for anything,' I exclaimed in delight, 'I'll answer for myself – I will be obedient, respectful . . . you know me . . .'

'It's precisely because I do know you that I'm inviting you to come tomorrow,' the girl said, laughing. 'I know you completely. But see that you come on the following condition: first (only be so kind as to do what I ask – you see, I'm speaking candidly), don't fall in love with me . . . That's impossible, I assure you. I'm prepared to be your friend, here's my hand . . . But falling in love is impossible, I beg you!'

'I swear,' I cried, as I clasped her hand . . .

'Come, come, don't swear, you see, I know that you're

capable of flaring up like gunpowder. Don't condemn me for speaking like this. If you only knew . . . I also have no one to whom I can say a word, from whom I can ask advice. Of course, the street is not the place to look for advisers, but you're an exception. I know you so well, as if we had been friends for twenty years . . . You won't betray me, will you? . . .'

'You'll see . . . Only I don't know how I'm going to survive the next twenty-four hours.'

'Sleep well; good night – and remember that I have already put myself into your hands. But your exclamation just now put it so nicely: must one really account for every feeling, even for brotherly sympathy! Do you know, that was put so nicely that I suddenly thought I might confide in you . . .'

'By all means, but about what? What's it about?'

'Until tomorrow. Let it be a secret in the meantime. It will be better for you that way; although from a distance it will look like a love story. Maybe I'll tell you tomorrow and maybe not . . . I'll talk with you a bit more first, we'll get to know each other better . . .'

'Oh, and tomorrow I'll tell you everything about myself! But what is this? It's as though a miracle were happening to me . . . My God, where am I? Well, tell me, aren't you glad that you didn't get angry as another woman would have done and drive me away from the very beginning? Two minutes and you have made me happy forever. Yes! happy; who knows, perhaps you have reconciled me with myself, resolved my doubts . . . Perhaps such moments overwhelm me . . . Well, I'll tell you everything tomorrow, you'll learn everything about me, everything . . .'

'Very well, I accept; and you'll start first . . .'

'Agreed.'

'Goodbye!'

'Goodbye!'

And we parted. I walked all night long; I couldn't make up my mind to go home. I was so happy . . . until tomorrow!

THE SECOND NIGHT

'Well, so you survived!' she said to me, laughing and taking hold of both my hands.

'I've been here for two hours already; you have no idea what I've been through today!'

'I know, I know . . . But now to the matter at hand. Do you know why I've come? Not to talk nonsense like yesterday, you know. Here's why: we need to act more sensibly from now on. I thought about all this for a long time last night.'

'But how, how are we to be more sensible? For my part, I'm ready; but really nothing more sensible has ever happened to me in all my life than what is happening now.'

'Is that so? First of all, please don't squeeze my hands like that; and second, I want to tell you that I thought about you long and hard today.'

'Well, and what conclusion did you reach?'

'Conclusion? I concluded that we must begin all over again, because today I came to the conclusion that I don't know you at all, that yesterday I acted like a child, like a little girl, and it goes without saying that it turned out that my kind heart was to blame for it all; that is, I praised

19

myself, which is how it always ends when we start examining our actions. And that's why, in order to correct this mistake, I've decided to find out everything I can about you in the most detailed manner. But since there's no one from whom I can find out anything about you, you must tell me everything yourself, everything that there is to know. Well, what sort of person are you? Quickly – begin, tell me the story of your life.'

'The story of my life!' I cried out, frightened. 'My story! But who told you that I have a story to tell? I don't have a story . . .'

'But how have you lived if there's no story?' she interrupted, smiling.

'Absolutely without stories of any kind! I lived, as they say, on my own, that is, absolutely alone – alone, completely alone – do you understand what it means to be alone?'

'But what do you mean by alone? Do you mean you never see anyone?'

'Oh, no, of course I see people, but nevertheless I am alone.'

'But can it really be that you don't talk to anyone?'

'Strictly speaking, to nobody.'

'So who are you, then, explain yourself! Wait, I'll hazard a guess: you probably have a grandmother, like I do. She's blind, and for as long as I can remember she has never let me go anywhere, so that I've practically forgotten how to talk. A couple of years ago I got into a lot of mischief and she saw that she couldn't control me, so she called me over and pinned my dress to hers with a safety pin – and ever since we sit like that for days on end; she knits a stocking, even though she's blind; and I sit beside her, sewing or reading a book to her out loud – it's such a strange way to live, and I've been pinned to her like that now for two years already . . .'

'Oh, my God, how dreadful! But no, I don't have a grandmother like that.'

'But if you don't, then how is it that you stay at home? . . .'

'Listen, do you want to know what sort of person I am?'

'Well, yes, yes!'

'In the strict sense of the word?'

'In the very strictest sense of the word!'

'Well, then, I'm a type.'

'Type, type! What sort of type?' the girl cried out, laughing as if she had not had a chance to laugh for a whole year. 'You're certainly very amusing company! Look: there's a bench here; let's sit down! No one walks by here, no one will hear us, and – you can begin your story! Because you won't succeed in persuading me otherwise, you do have a story, only you're concealing it. First of all, what is a type?'

'A type? A type is an eccentric, a ridiculous person!' I answered, and burst out laughing myself in response to her childish laughter. 'He's a real character. Listen: do you know what a dreamer is?'

'A dreamer? Excuse me, but of course I do! I'm a dreamer myself! What doesn't enter my head sometimes when I'm sitting beside my grandmother. Well, then you begin to dream, and you become so lost in your thoughts that before you know it you're marrying a Chinese prince . . . But sometimes dreaming is a good thing! But then, God only knows! Particularly if there's something to think about without dreaming,' the girl added, quite serious now.

'Excellent! If you've been married to a Chinese emperor, that means you'll understand me perfectly then. Well, listen . . . But excuse me; I don't even know your name.'

'At last! You certainly took your time about it!'

'Oh, my goodness! It never entered my head – I was so happy as it was . . .'

'My name is Nastenka.'

'Nastenka! And that's all?'

'That's all! Is that really not enough for you? What an insatiable fellow you are!'

'Not enough? On the contrary, it's a great deal, a very great deal indeed, Nastenka – you're a kind girl if you're Nastenka to me right away!'

'So, there you are!'

'So then, Nastenka, listen to what a ridiculous story this turns out to be.'

I sat down next to her, assumed a pedantically serious pose and began as though I were reading something that had been written down.

'There are, Nastenka, in case you don't know, there are rather strange little corners in Petersburg. It's as if the same sun that shines for all of Petersburg's people doesn't even peek into these places, but there is another different, new sun, as if specially ordered for these corners, and it shines on everything with a different, special light. In these corners, dear Nastenka, it's as if a completely different kind of life is lived, one that doesn't resemble that which seethes around us, but the kind that might exist in a faraway kingdom, and not among us in our serious, oh so serious times. And it is this life which is a mixture of something purely fantastic, fervently ideal, and at the same time (alas, Nastenka) dully prosaic and ordinary, not to say – incredibly vulgar.'

'Ugh! Good heavens! What an introduction! Whatever will I hear next?'

'You'll hear, Nastenka (it seems that I shall never tire of calling you Nastenka), you'll hear that in these corners live strange people – dreamers. A dreamer – if you require a precise definition – is not a man, but some sort of sexless being, you see. For the most part, he makes his home somewhere in an inaccessible corner, as if he were hiding there even from the light of day, and once he goes into hiding, he sticks to his corner, like a snail, or at any rate, he very much resembles in this regard that entertaining animal, both animal and house at the same time, which is called a tortoise. What do you think, why does he so love his own four walls, which are certain to be painted green, covered with soot, wretched and unforgivably grimy from tobacco smoke? Why does this ridiculous gentleman, when one of his few acquaintances comes to visit him (and he ends up losing all his acquaintances), why does this ridiculous person greet him with such embarrassment, such a changed countenance and such confusion, as though he had just committed a crime within his four walls, as though he had been forging counterfeit notes or some little poems to be sent to a journal with an anonymous letter in which it is revealed that a true poet has died and that his friend considers it his sacred duty to publish his ditties? Why, tell me, Nastenka, does the conversation between these two interlocutors never get going? Why does neither laughter nor some lively remark fly from the tongue of the completely unexpected and perplexed friend, who in different circumstances likes to laugh a great deal, as well as engage in lively banter, and conversations about the fair sex, and other cheerful subjects? And why, finally, does this friend, probably a recent acquaintance making his first visit – because in this case there will not be a second and the friend won't come again – why does this friend become so embarrassed, so stiff, all his wit notwithstanding (if indeed he has any) as he looks at the crestfallen face of his host, who in turn has already managed to become completely flustered and utterly muddled after gigantic but futile efforts to smooth over and keep the conversation going, to show his knowledge of the ways of the world, to talk, too, about the fair sex and, at the very least, by such deference to please the poor person who has turned up at the wrong place and mistakenly come to visit him? Why, finally, does the guest suddenly grab his hat and quickly leave, having remembered all of a sudden some very urgent business, which never existed, and somehow or other extricate his hand from the warm handshake of his host, who in every way possible was trying to show his regret and set right that which had been lost? Why does the departing friend chortle as he goes out the door, there and then vowing never to visit this crackpot, even though this crackpot is truly a most excellent fellow; at the same time why can he not deny his imagination the passing fancy of comparing, if only remotely, the physiognomy of his recent interlocutor throughout the entire time of their meeting with the look of an unhappy little kitten, treacherously captured by children who have mauled, frightened and tormented it in every way possible, and which has finally taken refuge from them under a chair, in the dark, and there for an entire hour at its leisure bristles, hisses and washes its aggrieved face with both paws, and for a long time afterwards looks with enmity at nature and life and even at the scraps from his master's dinner which the compassionate housekeeper had saved for him?'

'Listen,' interrupted Nastenka, who all this time had been listening to me in amazement, with her eyes and little mouth wide open. 'Listen: I absolutely do not know why all this happened and why you are putting such ridiculous questions to me; but what I do know for certain is that all these adventures certainly happened to you, word for word.'

'Without a doubt,' I answered with the most serious expression.

'Well, as there's no doubt, then continue,' Nastenka answered, 'because I very much want to know how it all ends.'

'You want to know, Nastenka, what our hero was doing in his corner – or rather, what I was doing, for the hero of this whole affair is myself – my own humble person; you want to know why I became so alarmed and was flustered for an entire day by the unexpected visit of a friend? You want to know why I was so startled, why I blushed so when the door to my room opened, why I didn't know how to receive my guest and why I floundered so shamefully under the weight of my own hospitality?'

'Well, yes, yes!' Nastenka answered. 'That's the whole point. Listen: you tell it splendidly, but could you tell it somehow less splendidly? Otherwise, you talk as though you were reading from a book.'

'Nastenka!' I answered in a dignified and stern voice, scarcely holding back my laughter, 'dear Nastenka, I know that I am telling it splendidly; I plead guilty – but I don't know how to tell it differently. Now, dear Nastenka, now I'm like King Solomon's genie trapped in an earthenware urn for a thousand years, under seven seals, and from which these seven seals were at last removed. Now, dear Nastenka, when we have come together again after such a lengthy separation – because I have known you for a long time, Nastenka, because I have long been searching for someone, and that is a sign that I was looking precisely for you and that we were fated to meet now – now in my head thousands of valves have opened and I must set loose this river of words, or I will choke to death. So then, I ask that you not interrupt me, Nastenka, but listen obediently and dutifully; otherwise – I'll keep my silence.'

'No-no-no! By no means! Speak! I won't say another word.'

'To continue: there is, my friend Nastenka, in my day one hour that I like exceedingly. It is the hour when almost all business, duties and engagements are coming to an end, and everybody is hurrying home to dinner, to lie down and rest, and there and then, as they're making their way home, they concoct other cheerful schemes pertaining to the evening, the night and all the rest of their free time. At this hour our hero, too – for allow me, Nastenka, to tell the story in the third person, because it's terribly embarrassing to tell all this in the first person – so then, at this hour our hero, too, who has also not been idle, walks along behind the others. But a strange sense of pleasure plays on his pale, somewhat rumpled face. With feeling he looks at the sunset, which slowly fades away in the cold Petersburg sky. When I say he looks, I'm lying: he doesn't look, but he contemplates it somehow without thinking, as if he were tired or pre-occupied at the same time with some other more interesting object, so that he can only cursorily, almost involuntarily, spare time for everything around him. He is pleased, because he has finished until tomorrow with the *business* that he finds irksome, and he is as happy as a schoolboy who has been dismissed from the classroom to his favourite games and mischief. Look at him in pro-file, Nastenka: you'll see at once that the joyful feeling fortunately has already begun to have an effect on his weak nerves and morbidly excited imagination. He's fallen deep in thought about something . . . Do you think it's about dinner? About this evening? What is he looking at like that? At that respectable-looking gentleman who bowed so picturesquely to the lady riding past him in a glittering carriage drawn by those frisky horses? No, Nastenka, what does he care now about such trifles? His *own particular* life has already made him rich; he some-how suddenly became rich, and not in vain did the farewell ray of the dying sun so gaily sparkle before him and call forth an entire swarm of impressions from his warmed heart. Now he scarcely notices the path on which even the most petty trifle would have struck him earlier. Now the "Goddess of Fantasy" (if you have read Zhukov-sky, dear Nastenka) has already spun her golden warp and begun to fashion before his eyes patterns of a fan-tastic, marvellous life – and who knows, perhaps with her whimsical hand she has transported him to the seventh crystal heaven from the excellent granite sidewalk on which he was walking home. Try stopping him now, and ask him suddenly where he's standing now, along which streets has he walked. He probably will remember nothing, neither where he was walking, nor where he is now standing, and after blushing with vexation he will certainly tell some lie in order to save face. That's why he was so taken aback, almost crying out and looking all around in alarm, when a very respectable old woman who had lost her way politely stopped him in the middle of the sidewalk and began to ask him for directions. Frowning with vexation, he carries on walking, scarcely noticing that he has caused more than one passer-by to smile and turn round to look at him as he walked away, and that some little girl, as she timidly made way for him, began to laugh loudly, as she looked wide-eyed at his broad, contemplative smile and gesturing hands. But the same fantasy caught up in its playful flight the old woman, and the curious passers-by, and the laughing girl, and the peasants who were spending their night right there on the barges that crowded the Fontanka (let's suppose that at this moment our hero was walking along there), and mischievously wove everybody and everything into its canvas, like a fly in a spider's web, and with this new acquisition the eccentric had entered his comforting lair, sat down to dinner, finished his dinner long ago and only came to when the pensive and eternally doleful Matryona

29

who waits on him had already cleared everything from the table and given him his pipe; he came to and recalled with surprise that he had already had his dinner, but had taken no notice whatsoever how that was accomplished. It had grown dark in the room; his heart feels empty and forlorn; the whole kingdom of dream has collapsed around him, collapsed without a trace, without a sound or fuss – it flew past like a vision, and he himself doesn't remember what he was dreaming about. But some vague sensation faintly disturbs his breast and causes it to ache, some new desire seductively tickles and excites his fancy and imperceptibly summons a whole swarm of new phantoms. Quiet reigns in the little room; solitude and indolence caress the imagination; it faintly catches fire, it is faintly brought to the boil, like the water in the coffeepot of old Matryona, who placidly potters about next door in the kitchen, as she makes her cook's coffee. Now it's already gently breaking through in bursts; now the book, picked up without purpose and at random, is already falling from my dreamer's hand, without his even getting to the third page. His imagination is once again incited, excited, and suddenly again a new world, a new enchanting life with its glistening vistas flashes before him. A new dream is new happiness! A new dose of exquisite, voluptuous poison! Oh, what does real life have to offer him! In his misdirected view, you and I, Nastenka, live so idly, slowly, sluggishly; in his view, we are all so dissatisfied with our fate, so worn down by our life!

And really, as a matter of fact, look how everything at first glance among us is cold, gloomy, indeed wrathful . . . "The poor things," my dreamer thinks. And it's no wonder that he should think so! Look at these magical phantoms that so enchantingly, so whimsically, so boundlessly and broadly take shape before him in such a magical, animated picture, in which the most important figure in the foreground, of course, is he himself, our dreamer, his own dear person. Look, what diverse adventures, what an endless swarm of ecstatic daydreams. You will ask, perhaps, what does he dream about? Why ask that? About everything . . . about the role of the poet, who at first goes unrecognized, but is later crowned with success; about friendship with Hoffmann; St Bartholomew's Night, Diana Vernon, the heroic role of Ivan Vasilyevich in the taking of Kazan, Clara Mowbray, Effie Deans, the Council of the Prelates and Huss before them, the rising of the dead in *Robert* (do you remember the music? It smells of the graveyard!), Minna and Brenda, the battle of Beryozina, the reading of a poem at Countess V.D.'s, Danton, Cleopatra *ei suoi amanti*, the little house in Kolomna; his own little corner, with a dear creature at his side who listens on a winter's evening, with her little mouth and eyes open, just as you're listening to me now, my little angel . . . No, Nastenka, what need has he, this voluptuous sluggard, of this life that you and I desire so? He thinks that this is a poor, pitiful life, not anticipating that perhaps some day the sad hour will strike for him as well, when for a single day of this pitiful life he would give up all of his fantastic years, and give them up not for joy, or for happiness, and without wishing to choose in this hour of sadness, repentance and boundless sorrow. But this terrible time has yet to come – he desires nothing, because he is above desire, because he has everything, because he is sated, because he himself is the artist of his life and he creates it for himself every hour to suit his latest whim. And, you see, this fairy-tale, fantastic world is created so easily, so naturally! As though all this were truly not a phantom! Indeed, he is prepared to believe at certain moments that all of this life is not the excitement of feelings, not a mirage, not a delusion of the imagination, but that it is, indeed, authentic, genuine, real! Why, tell me, Nastenka, oh why, at such moments does one's breathing become laboured? Why, by what magic, by what mysterious caprice does the pulse quicken, do tears gush forth from the dreamer's eyes, his pale, moist cheeks burn as his entire being fills with such irresistible delight? Why do whole sleepless nights pass by like a single instant in inexhaustible merriment and happiness, and when the dawn's rosy ray shines through the windows and the daybreak illumines the gloomy room with its dubious fantastic light, such as we have in Petersburg, why does our dreamer, exhausted and weary, throw himself on his bed and fall asleep, his tormented and overwhelmed spirit trembling with ecstasy, while his heart aches with a sweet agony? Yes, Nastenka, you deceive yourself, and unwittingly and dispassionately believe that it is a genuine, true passion that disturbs his soul, you unwittingly believe that there is something alive and tangible in his incorporeal daydreams! But, you see, it's all a delusion – take, for example, the love that has pierced his breast with all its inexhaustible joy, with all its wearisome torments . . . Just look at him and you'll be convinced! Would you believe, when you look at him, dear Nastenka, that indeed he has never known her whom he loves so in his frenzied daydreams? Can it be that he has only seen her in certain captivating phantoms and only dreamed this passion? Can it really be that they have not spent so many years of their lives together hand in hand – alone, just the two of them, having forsaken the entire world and each uniting their life, their world, with the life of their friend? Can it really be that at this late hour, when the time had come to part, she did not lay there, sobbing and grieving on his breast, not hearing the storm, which was breaking under the bleak sky, or the wind, which plucked and carried away the tears from her black lashes? Can this really all have been a dream – this garden, cheerless, desolate and wild, with paths overgrown with moss, secluded, and gloomy, where they so often would walk together, where they hoped, grieved, loved, loved each other for such a long time, "so long and tenderly"? And this strange, ancestral home, in which she had lived for such a long time, secluded and melancholy, with her sullen, old husband, always silent and peevish, who frightened them, while they, timid as children, dolefully and timorously concealed their love from each other? How they suffered, how fearful they were, and how innocent and pure was their love and how (it goes without saying, Nastenka) malicious people were! And, my God, was it really not she he met later, far from the shores of their homeland, under an alien sky, in the torrid South, in the marvellous Eternal City, in the brilliance of a ball, to the thunder of music, in a palazzo (it absolutely must be a palazzo), drowned in a sea of lights, on this balcony, wreathed with myrtle and roses, where she, upon recognizing him, so hastily took off her mask and whispered: "I am free", and trembling, threw herself into his arms, and with a cry of rapture, they embraced, and in an instant they forgot sorrow, separation, all their torments, the gloomy house, the old man, the dismal garden in their distant homeland, the bench on which, with one last passionate kiss, she had torn herself away from his arms, numb from torments of despair? . . . Oh, you must agree, Nastenka, that you would be startled, feel embarrassed and blush like a schoolboy who had just crammed into his pocket an apple stolen from the neighbour's orchard, if some lanky, hearty lad, a merry fellow and a joker, your uninvited friend, opened your door and shouted out, as if nothing had happened: "And I, my dear fellow, just got back from Pavlovsk!" My goodness! The old count has died, ineffable happiness is close at hand – and here people are coming from Pavlovsk!'

I pathetically fell silent, upon concluding my pathetic exclamations. I remember that I wanted terribly somehow to force myself to burst out laughing, because I already sensed that a hostile little demon had begun to stir inside me, that I was about to choke, that my chin was beginning to quiver and that my eyes were watering more and more . . . I expected Nastenka, who was listening to me with her intelligent eyes wide open, to burst into her childish, irrepressibly merry laughter, and was already regretting that I had gone too far, that I had been wrong to tell her about what had long seethed in my heart, about which I could talk as though I were reading a written text, because I had long ago passed sentence on myself and now could not resist reading it, to confess, without expecting that I should be understood; but to my surprise, she kept silent; after waiting a little bit she gently pressed my hand and with a timid concern asked:

'Can you really have lived your whole life like that?'

'My whole life, Nastenka,' I replied, 'my whole life and I believe that's how I'll end my days!'

'No, that's impossible,' she said uneasily, 'it won't be like that – that would mean I would likely live out my whole life by Grandmother's side. Listen, you do know that it's bad for you to live like that?'

'I know, Nastenka, I know!' I exclaimed, no longer holding my feelings in check. 'And now I know more than ever that I've wasted all my best years for nothing! I know this now, and I feel it all the more painfully now

35

that I see that God himself has sent you, my good angel, to me, in order to tell me this and prove it to me. As I sit beside you and talk to you now, I'm terrified even to think about the future, because the future is once again loneliness, once again this stagnant, useless life; and what will there be for me to dream about when I have already been so happy in real life beside you! Oh, bless you, dear girl, for not turning me away from the very first, for making it possible that I can now say that I have lived at least two evenings in my life!'

'Oh, no, no!' Nastenka cried out, and little tears began to glisten in her eyes. 'No, it won't be like that any more; we won't part like that! What are two evenings!'

'Oh, Nastenka, Nastenka! Do you know you have reconciled me with myself for a good long time? Do you know that now I will not think so badly of myself as I sometimes have done? Do you know that now, perhaps, I will no longer suffer anguish for having committed a crime and sin in my life, because a life like that is a crime and sin? And don't think that I have been exaggerating anything to you, for God's sake, Nastenka, don't think that, because sometimes I am overcome by moments of such anguish, such anguish . . . Because at those moments it begins to seem that I will never be able to begin living a real life; because it already seems that I have lost all sense, all feeling for the genuine, the real; because, in the end, I curse myself; because after my fantastic nights I am visited by sobering moments that are horrible!

Meanwhile, you hear all around you how the throng of humanity thunders and spins in the whirlwind of life; you hear, you see how people live – they live in reality; you see that life for them is not forbidden, that their life doesn't vanish like a dream, like a vision, that their life is eternally renewing, eternally young, and not a single hour of it resembles any other; whereas how cheerless and monotonously banal is the timorous fantasy, the slave of a shadow, of an idea, the slave of the first cloud that suddenly obscures the sun and fills with anguish the heart of every true Petersburger, which holds its sun so dear – but what sort of fantasy is there to be found in anguish! You sense that this *inexhaustible fantasy* is finally growing tired, that it is becoming exhausted under constant strain; because, you see, you are growing into manhood, you are outgrowing your former ideals: they are being smashed to dust, to bits and pieces; and if there is no other life, then you must build it from these bits and pieces. But meanwhile your soul yearns and pleads for something else! And in vain does the dreamer rake through his old dreams, as if they were ashes, searching in these ashes for at least some little spark, in order to fan it into flames, and with this rekindled fire warm his heart, which has grown cold, and resurrect in himself once again everything that he had held dear, that had touched his soul, that had made his blood boil, that had brought tears to his eyes and had so splendidly deceived him! Do you know, Nastenka, how low I have fallen? Do you know that I'm compelled now to celebrate the anniversary of my own sensations, the anniversary of that which was formerly so dear, of that which in essence never took place – because this anniversary is celebrated in honour of those same foolish, phantom dreams – and to do it because even those foolish dreams are no more, because I have nothing with which to replenish them: you see, even dreams need to be replenished! Do you know that I now like to recall and visit at certain times places where I was once happy in my own way, I like to fashion my present so that it's in harmony with the irrevocable past, and I often wander like a shadow, without need or purpose, downcast and sad, through the alleys and streets of Petersburg? And what memories! You recall, for instance, that exactly a year ago now, exactly at this very same time, at this very same hour, you wandered along this very sidewalk just as lonely, just as downcast as you are now! And you recall that your dreams were sad then as well, and even though it was not better then, nevertheless, you somehow feel that it was easier, that you lived more comfortably, that there wasn't this black brooding that troubles you now; that you didn't have these pangs of conscience, these gloomy, dismal pangs that now give you no peace night or day. And you ask yourself: Where are your dreams? And you shake your head and say: How quickly do the years fly by! And again you ask yourself: What have you done with your years? Where have you buried your best days? Did you live or not? Look, you say to yourself, look how cold the world is becoming. More years will pass, followed by gloomy solitude, and then doddering old age will come on a walking-stick, to be followed by anguish and despondency. Your fantastic world will grow pale, your dreams will wither, die and scatter like yellow leaves from the trees . . . Oh, Nastenka! It will be sad, you know, to be left alone, quite alone, and not even have something to regret – nothing, absolutely nothing . . . because all that I have lost, all this, it was all nothing, a stupid, round zero – it was merely a dream!'

'Now, stop trying to make me feel sorry for you!' Nastenka said, wiping away a tear which had rolled down from her eye. 'That's all over now! The two of us will be together now; now, no matter what happens to me, we will never part. Listen. I'm a simple girl, without much education, although my grandmother did hire a teacher for me; but I truly do understand you, because everything that you've told me just now, I experienced myself when Grandmother pinned me to her dress. Of course, I couldn't have told it so well as you have done; I'm not educated,' she added timidly, because she was still feeling some sort of respect for my pathetic speech and my lofty style, 'but I'm very happy that you have confided in me so completely. Now I know you, through and through, I know everything about you. And do you know what? I want to tell you my story now, all of it, frankly, and afterwards you'll give me your advice. You're a very sensible man; do you promise to give me your advice?'

'Ah, Nastenka,' I replied, 'although I've never been an adviser, much less a sensible adviser, I see now that it would somehow be very sensible if we were to always live like this, and we would give each other a lot of sensible advice! Well, my pretty Nastenka, what advice should I give you? Tell me frankly; I'm so cheerful, happy, bold and sensible now that I won't be at a loss for words.'

'No, no,' Nastenka interrupted, laughing, 'it's not only sensible advice that I need; I need advice that is heartfelt and brotherly, as though you had loved me all your life!'

'All right, Nastenka, all right!' I cried out in delight, 'and if I'd already loved you for twenty years, I still couldn't have loved you more than I do right now!'

'Give me your hand!' Nastenka said.

'Here it is!' I answered, as I gave her my hand.

'And so, let's begin my story!'

NASTENKA'S STORY

'Half of my story you already know, that is, you know that I have an old grandmother . . .'

'If the other half is as short as this one . . .' I interrupted, laughing.

'Keep quiet and listen. First of all, a condition: you're not to interrupt me, or else I'll very likely get muddled. Now, listen quietly.

'I have an old grandmother. I found myself with her when I was still a very little girl, because my mother and father had died. It's fair to suppose that Grandmother had been richer at one time, because even now she recalls better days. It was she who taught me French and then later hired a teacher for me. When I was fifteen years old (I'm seventeen now), the lessons stopped. And it was at this time that I got into a lot of mischief; but I won't tell you what I did; it's enough to say that my misdeed was minor. But Grandmother called me one morning and said that since she was blind she couldn't keep an eye on me, so she took a pin and fastened my dress to hers, and then she said that we would sit like that for the rest of our lives if, of course, I didn't behave better. In a word, at first it was quite impossible to get away: I did all my work, reading and studying right beside Grandmother. I once tried to trick her and talked Fyokla into sitting in my place. Fyokla is our maid, she's deaf. Fyokla sat down instead of me; Grandmother had fallen asleep in her armchair at the time, and I set off for my girlfriend's not far away. Well, it ended badly. Grandmother woke up when I was away and asked about something, thinking that I was still sitting quietly in my place. Fyokla could see that Grandmother was asking for something, but she couldn't hear what it was, she thought and thought about what she should do, undid the pin, and took to her heels . . .'

Here Nastenka paused and laughed. I started to laugh with her. She stopped at once.

'Now listen, don't you laugh at my grandmother. I'm laughing, because it's funny . . . What can I do when Grandmother really is like that, but I love her all the same. Well, that time I certainly got what for: I was sat down in my place at once and wasn't allowed to budge an inch.

'Oh, yes, I also forgot to tell you that we have, that is, Grandmother has her own house, that is, a tiny little house, with only three windows, all made of wood and as old as Grandmother herself; and there's an attic upstairs; and so a new lodger moved into our attic . . .'

'Consequently, there must have been an old lodger?' I noted in passing.

'Well, of course there was,' Nastenka replied, 'and one who knew how to keep quiet better than you do. True, he could barely move his tongue. He was a little old man, withered, mute, blind, lame, so that it finally became impossible for him to live in this world, and he died; then we needed a new lodger, because we can't live without a lodger: that together with Grandmother's pension is practically our entire income. The new lodger, as luck would have it, was a young man, not from around here, from out of town. Since he didn't try to bargain with her, Grandmother took him in, but later she asked: "So, Nastenka, is our lodger young or not?" I didn't want to lie: "Now," I say, "Grandmother, it's not as though he's very young, but then he's not an old man." "Well, and is he good-looking?" Grandmother asks.

'Again, I don't wish to lie. "Yes," I say, "he's good-looking, Grandmother!" And Grandmother says: "Oh, what a nuisance, what a nuisance! I'm saying this, Granddaughter, so that you don't get carried away by him. Oh, what times we live in! Who would have thought it possible, such a piddling lodger – and he has to be good-looking as well: things were different in the old days!"

'It's always the old days with Grandmother! She was younger in the old days, and the sun was warmer in the old days, and cream didn't go sour so quickly in the old days – it's always the old days! And so I sit and keep quiet, and think to myself: why is Grandmother filling my head with ideas and asking whether our lodger is handsome or whether he's young? But that was all there was to it; I just gave it a thought and there and then began counting my stitches again – I was knitting stockings – and then completely forgot about it.

'And then one morning the lodger came to ask about his room being wallpapered as he had been promised. One thing led to another, Grandmother is talkative, you see, and she says: "Go to my bedroom, Nastenka, and bring me my accounts." I immediately jumped up, blushing, I don't know why, and I'd forgotten that I was sitting there pinned to Grandmother; I didn't quietly unpin myself so that the lodger wouldn't see, no – I dashed off so that Grandmother's chair went flying. When I saw that the lodger now knew everything about me, I blushed, stood there as if I were rooted to the ground and burst into tears – I became so ashamed and miserable at that moment that life didn't seem worth living! Grandmother shouts: "Why are you just standing there?" – which made me cry even more . . . When the lodger saw this, when he saw that I was embarrassed on account of him, he took his leave and went away at once!

'From that moment on I would practically die at the slightest sound in the entrance hall. There goes the lodger, I'd say to myself, and quietly undo the pin just in case. Only it was never him, he never came. Two weeks passed; the lodger sent word through Fyokla that he had a lot of French books and that they were all good books, suitable for me to read; wouldn't Grandmother like me to read them to her, so that we wouldn't be bored? Grandmother accepted with gratitude, but she kept asking if the books were moral or not, because if the books were immoral, then you, Nastenka, she says, mustn't read them under any circumstances, you'll learn bad things.

'"And what would I learn, Grandmother? What's written in them?"

'"Oh!" she says, "they describe how young men lead well-behaved girls astray; how under the pretence of wanting to marry them, they carry them off from their parents' house; how they later abandon these unfortunate girls to the whims of fate; and how they then perish in the most lamentable manner. I," Grandmother says, "have read a lot of books like that and everything," she says, "is so wonderfully described that you sit up all night, quietly reading. So you, Nastenka," she says, "see that you don't read them. What kind of books," she asks, "has he sent?"

'"They're all novels by Walter Scott, Grandmother."

'"Novels by Walter Scott! But wait just a minute, there must be some sort of shenanigans going on here. Take a good look to see if he slipped a little love note in one of them."

'"No, I say, Grandmother, there isn't a note."

'"And look under the binding as well; sometimes they stuff it into the binding, the rascals! . . ."

'"No, Grandmother, there isn't anything under the binding either."

'"Well, what did I tell you!"

'And so we began to read Walter Scott and in a month

45

or so we had read almost half. Then he sent us some more and some more. He sent Pushkin; in the end I couldn't be without a book and stopped thinking about marrying a Chinese prince.

'That's how things stood when I chanced to meet our lodger on the staircase. Grandmother had sent me for something. He stopped, I blushed and he blushed; he laughed though, said hello, asked after Grandmother's health and says: "So have you read the books?" I answered: "Yes." "Which one," he asks, "did you like the most?" And I say: "I liked *Ivanhoe* and Pushkin best of all." And that was the end of it that time.

'A week later I ran into him again on the staircase. This time Grandmother hadn't sent me, I had needed to get something for myself. It was after two, which was when the lodger would come home. "Hello!" he says. I answer: "Hello!"

'"Don't you get bored," he asks, "sitting with your grandmother all day long?"

'As soon as he asked me that, I blushed, I don't know why; I became embarrassed, and once again my feelings were hurt, evidently because now others had begun asking questions about this. I wanted to walk away without answering, but I didn't have the strength.

'"Listen," he says, "you're a good girl! Forgive me for talking with you like this, but I assure you I wish you well more than your grandmother does. Don't you have any girlfriends whom you can go and visit?"

'I say that I don't have any, that there was one, Mashenka, but that she's gone away to Pskov.

'"Listen," he says, "would you like to go to the theatre with me?"

'"To the theatre? But what about Grandmother?"

'"Well," he says, "you can go without telling her . . ."

'"No," I say, "I don't want to deceive Grandmother. Goodbye!"

'"Well, goodbye," he says, and he didn't say another word.

'Only after dinner he comes to see us; he sat down, talked with Grandmother for a long time, asked whether she goes out anywhere, whether she has any friends – and suddenly he says: "I took a box at the opera today; they're putting on *The Barber of Seville*, friends wanted to go and then cancelled, so I'm left with the tickets."

'"*The Barber of Seville*!" Grandmother exclaimed, "is that the same *Barber* they used to put on in the old days?"

'"Yes," he says, "it's the very same *Barber*," and he cast a glance at me. And then I understood everything, blushed and my heart began to thump in expectation!

'"But of course I know it!" Grandmother says. "In the old days I even sang Rosina in amateur theatricals."

'"So, would you like to go today?" said the lodger. "My tickets will go to waste."

'"Yes, I suppose we could go," Grandmother says, "why shouldn't we go? After all, my Nastenka has never been to the theatre."

'My goodness, what joy! We at once pulled ourselves together, got ready and set off. Even though Grandmother is blind, she still wanted to hear the music, and besides she's a kind old woman: more than anything she wanted me to enjoy myself; we should never have gone on our own. I won't tell you my impressions of *The Barber of Seville*, except to say that all that evening our lodger looked at me so nicely, and spoke so nicely that I saw at once that he had wanted to test me in the morning by proposing that I go with him alone. Well, what joy! I went to bed so proud, so happy; my heart was pounding so that I became slightly feverish and I raved on about *The Barber of Seville* all night long.

'I thought that he would stop by more and more often after that – but that wasn't the case. He almost stopped coming altogether. And so, he would drop by once a month, and then only to invite us to the theatre. We went with him again a couple of times. Only I wasn't at all happy with this. I saw that he simply felt sorry for me, because I was kept under Grandmother's thumb so, and there wasn't anything else to it. And then as time went on something came over me: I couldn't sit still, and I couldn't read, and I couldn't work; sometimes I would laugh and do something to Grandmother out of spite, while at other times I would simply cry. In the end, I grew thin and almost became ill. The opera season was over and the lodger stopped dropping by altogether; whenever we would meet – always on that same staircase, it goes without saying – he would bow so silently, so seriously, as though he didn't wish to speak, and then walk down all the way to the front door, while I was still standing halfway up the stairs, as red as a cherry, because all my blood would rush to my head whenever we met.

'Now we're coming to the end. Exactly a year ago, in May, the lodger comes to us and tells Grandmother that he has finished all his business and that he must return to Moscow for a year. When I heard this I turned white and collapsed on to the chair half dead. Grandmother didn't notice anything, and after announcing that he was going away, he took his leave and left.

'What was I to do? I thought and thought, I became more and more miserable, and finally I came to a decision. He was to leave the next day, and I decided that I would bring everything to a conclusion that evening after Grandmother had gone to bed. And that's what happened. I gathered into a bundle all my dresses, as many underclothes as was necessary, and with the bundle in hand, neither dead nor alive, I set off to our lodger's room in the attic. I think I spent an entire hour walking up that staircase. When I opened his door, he cried out upon seeing me. He thought that I was a ghost, and rushed to get me some water, because I could scarcely stand on my own feet. My heart was pounding so that my head ached and my thinking had become confused. When I came to my senses, I began straightaway by placing my bundle on his bed, sat down next to it, buried my face in my hands and let loose floods of tears. He seemed to understand everything in an instant and stood before me pale, looking at me with such sadness that it broke my heart.

'"Listen," he began, "listen, Nastenka, I can't do anything; I'm a poor man; I don't have anything yet, not even a decent job; how would we live if I were to marry you?"

'We talked for a long time, but in the end I worked myself into such a state that I said I couldn't live with Grandmother, that I would run away from her, that I didn't want to be pinned to her and that if he liked, I would go with him to Moscow, because I couldn't live without him. Shame, and love, and pride spoke in me all at once, and I collapsed on his bed almost in convulsions. I was so afraid of a refusal!

'He sat in silence for several minutes, then got up, walked over to me and took me by the hand.

'"Listen, my dear, my sweet Nastenka!" he began, also through tears. "Listen, I swear to you that if ever I am in the position to marry, then you will certainly be the one to make me happy; I assure you that now only you alone can make me happy. Listen: I am going to Moscow and will stay there for exactly one year. I hope to put my affairs in order. When I return, and if you have not stopped loving me, then I swear to you that we will be happy. But this is impossible now; I can't, I don't even have the right to promise something. But, I repeat, if this doesn't happen in a year's time, then it certainly will some day; it goes without saying – but only in the event that you don't prefer somebody else to me, because I cannot and dare not bind you by any sort of promise."

'That's what he told me and the next day he went away. We both agreed not to say a word about this to Grandmother. That was how he wanted it. Well, now my story is almost finished. Exactly a year has passed. He has arrived, he has been here already three whole days and, and . . .'

'And what?' I cried out, impatient to hear the end.

'And he still hasn't shown himself!' Nastenka answered, as if summoning up all her strength. 'There has been neither hide nor hair of him . . .'

Here she stopped, fell silent for a bit, bent her head and suddenly, having covered her face with her hands, began to sob so hard that it broke my heart.

I wasn't at all expecting an ending like that.

'Nastenka!' I began in a timid and ingratiating voice, 'Nastenka! For goodness' sake, don't cry! How do you know? Maybe he hasn't arrived yet . . .'

'He's here, he's here!' Nastenka rejoined. 'He's here, I know it. We made an agreement back then, on that evening before his departure: when we had already said everything that I've told you, and we had come to an agreement, we came out here for a stroll, right on this very embankment. It was ten o'clock; we were sitting on this bench; I had stopped crying, and I was enjoying listening to him talk . . . He said that upon his arrival he would come to us at once and if I didn't refuse him, then we would tell Grandmother about everything. Now he's arrived, I know it, and he hasn't come, he hasn't!'

And once again she broke down in tears.

'Good heavens! Is there really nothing I can do to ease your sorrow?' I cried out, jumping up from the bench in despair. 'Tell me, Nastenka, couldn't I at least go and see him?'

'Would that really be possible?' she said, suddenly raising her head.

'No, of course not, no!' I said, after giving it some thought. 'But here's what you could do – write a letter.'

'No, that's impossible, I couldn't do that,' she answered resolutely, but she had already lowered her head and wasn't looking at me.

'How is it that you can't? Why can't you?' I continued, taking up my idea. 'But you know, Nastenka, you need a certain kind of letter! There are letters and then there are letters and . . . Oh, Nastenka, it's true! Believe me, believe me! I wouldn't give you bad advice. All this can be arranged! It was you who took the first step – then why can't you now . . .'

'I can't, I can't! It would seem that I was forcing myself on him . . .'

'Oh, my dear little Nastenka!' I interrupted, not concealing a smile, 'not at all, no; you, of course, have a right

to, because he promised you. And everything tells me
that he's a delicate person, that he conducted himself
properly,' I continued, becoming more and more enrap-
tured with the logic of my own arguments and convictions.
'How did he conduct himself? He bound himself with a
promise. He said that he would not marry anyone but
you, if he does marry; he left you completely free to refuse
him even now ... Under such circumstances, you may
take the first step, you have the right, you have the advantage over him, if, for example, you should wish to release
him from his promise ...'

'Listen, how would you write it?'

'What?'

'Why, this letter.'

'I would write it like this: "Dear Sir ..."'

'Is this "Dear Sir" absolutely necessary?'

'Absolutely! But then again, why should it be? I
suppose ...'

'Well, well! Go on!'

'"Dear Sir! Forgive me for ..." But no, we don't need
any forgiveness! Here the fact itself justifies everything;
write simply:

I am writing you. Forgive my impatience; but for a whole
year hope alone has made me happy; am I to blame that
I cannot now bear even a day of doubt? Now, when you
have come back, perhaps you have changed your inten-
tions. Then this letter will tell you that I do not complain,

nor do I blame you. I do not blame you that I have no power over your heart; such, then, is my fate!

You are a noble person. You will not laugh and will not be annoyed at my impatient lines. Remember that they are written by a poor girl, that she is alone, that she has no one to teach her or to advise her and that she has never been able to control her heart. But forgive me that doubt should have crept into my heart for even a single moment. You are not capable of insulting, even in thought, the one who loved you so and who still loves you.'

'Yes, yes! That's exactly what I was thinking!' Nastenka cried out, and joy began to shine in her eyes. 'Oh, you have resolved my doubts, God himself has sent you to me! Thank you, thank you!'

'For what? For God sending me?' I answered, gazing in delight at her happy little face.

'Yes, for that as well.'

'Oh, Nastenka! You know, we thank some people for merely living at the same time as we do. I thank you for the fact that I met you, that I will remember you for all my life!'

'Well, enough, enough! And now look here, listen closely: we agreed then that as soon as he arrived, he would immediately let me know, that he would leave a letter for me at a certain place, with some acquaintances of mine, good and simple people who know nothing about this; or that if he couldn't write me a letter, because you can't always say everything in a letter, then the very same day that he arrived he would be here at exactly ten o'clock, where we arranged to meet. I know that he's arrived; but it's now the third day and there's been no letter, and he hasn't come. It's quite impossible for me to get away from my grandmother in the morning. Tomorrow, give my letter to these same good people, about whom I just told you: they will forward it; and if there's an answer, then you bring it yourself in the evening at ten o'clock.'

'But the letter, the letter! After all, you need to write the letter! So this will all probably be the day after tomorrow.'

'The letter . . .' Nastenka answered, a bit confused, 'the letter . . . but . . .'

But she didn't complete her thought. At first she turned her little face away from me, blushed, like a rose, and suddenly I felt in my hand a letter that had evidently been written long ago, sealed and all ready to go. Some familiar, sweet, graceful recollection passed through my mind!

'R, o-Ro, s, i-si, n, a-na,' I began.

'Rosina!' we both began singing – I, almost embracing her in delight, and she, having blushed as only she could blush, laughing through her tears, which trembled like pearls on her black eyelashes.

'Well, enough, enough! Goodbye now!' she said in a

rush. 'Here's the letter for you, and here's the address to take it to. Goodbye! Until we meet! Until tomorrow!'

She firmly clasped both my hands, nodded her head and flew away like an arrow down the lane. I stood there for a long time, following her with my eyes.

'Until tomorrow! Until tomorrow!' flashed through my head, as she disappeared from sight.

THE THIRD NIGHT

Today was a sad, rainy day, without a ray of hope, just like my future old age. I am besieged by such strange thoughts, such dark sensations, such obscure questions, which still crowd my mind – and somehow I have neither the strength nor the desire to resolve them. It is not for me to resolve all this!

Today we will not see each other. Yesterday, when we were saying goodbye, clouds began to gather in the sky and a mist was rising. I said that tomorrow the weather would be bad; she didn't answer, she didn't want to say anything that would go contrary to her wishes; for her this day was to be both bright and clear, and there wasn't to be a single cloud to darken her happiness.

'If it rains, then we won't see each other!' she said. 'I won't come.'

I thought that she wouldn't notice the rain today, but she didn't come.

Yesterday was our third meeting, our third white night . . .

But how fine joy and happiness make a person! How the heart seethes with love! It seems that you want to pour out all your heart into another's heart, you want everything to be gay, laughter everywhere. And how infectious is this joy! Yesterday in her words there was such tenderness, so much heartfelt kindness towards me . . . How she flattered me, how she treated me with affection, how she cheered and pampered my heart! Oh, how much coquetry springs forth from happiness! And I . . . I took everything for the genuine article; I thought that she . . .

But, my goodness! How could I have thought that? How could I have been so blind, when everything had already been taken by another, when everything was not mine, when, in the end, even this very tenderness of hers, her attentions, her love . . . yes, her love for me – was nothing more than joy at the impending meeting with someone else, the desire to thrust her happiness on me? . . . When he didn't come, when we waited in vain, she frowned, lost heart and became frightened. All her movements, all her words were no longer so light, playful and gay. And, strangely enough, she doubled her attentions to me as if instinctively wishing to lavish upon me all that she wished for herself, and that she feared might not come to pass. My Nastenka was so timid, so afraid, that it seems she understood at last that I loved her, and she took pity on my poor love. And so it is that when we are unhappy we more strongly feel the unhappiness of others; feeling is not shattered, but becomes concentrated . . .

I had come to her with a full heart, scarcely able to wait for our meeting. I had no presentiment of how I would feel now, no presentiment it would all end differently. She was beaming with joy, she was waiting for her answer. He himself was the answer. He was supposed to come, to come running at her summons. She came a whole hour earlier than I. At first she shrieked with laughter at everything, laughed at my every word. I was just about to speak and fell silent.

'Do you know why I'm so happy?' she said, 'so happy to look at you? Why I love you so today?'

'Well?' I asked, and my heart began to tremble.

'I love you because you didn't fall in love with me. Why, someone else in your place would have started bothering me, pestering me, sighing, falling ill, but you're such a dear!'

And then she squeezed my hand so that I almost cried out. She laughed.

'My goodness! What a friend you are!' she began a minute later very seriously. 'Yes, God himself sent you to me! Well, what would have happened to me if you had not been with me now? You're so unselfish! You love me so! When I'm married, we will be great friends, more than if we had been brothers. I will love you almost as much as I love him . . .'

I began to feel somehow terribly sad at that moment; however, something very much like laughter was beginning to stir in my soul.

'You're nervous,' I said, 'you're afraid; you think that he won't come.'

'Good heavens!' she answered, 'if I were any less happy, I should probably burst into tears on account of your lack of faith, your reproaches. However, you've given me an idea and a lot to think about; but I'll think about it later, and now I'll confess to you that you spoke the truth! Yes, I'm somehow not myself; I'm somehow all wrapped up in expectations and somehow feel everything too lightly. But enough, let's not talk about feelings! . . .'

At that moment steps could be heard, and in the darkness appeared a passer-by who was walking in our direction. We both began to tremble; she almost cried out. I let go of her hand and made a gesture as though I wanted to walk away. But we were both mistaken: it was not he.

'What are you afraid of? Why did you stop holding my hand?' she said as she gave it to me again. 'Well, what's the matter? We'll meet him together. I want him to see that we love each other.'

'That we love each other!' I cried.

'Oh, Nastenka, Nastenka!' I thought to myself. 'How much you've said with that one word. Such a love, Nastenka, at *certain* moments can make the heart grow cold and make one miserable. Your hand is cold, mine is as hot as fire. How blind you are, Nastenka! . . . Oh, how unbearable is the happy person at certain moments! But I couldn't be angry with you! . . .'

Finally, my heart was overflowing.

'Listen, Nastenka!' I cried, 'do you know what I've been through today?'

'Well, what, what is it? Tell me quickly! Why have you been silent all this time!'

'First of all, Nastenka, when I had carried out all your commissions, delivered the letter, visited your good people, then . . . then I returned home and went to bed.'

'Is that all?' she interrupted, laughing.

'Yes, almost all,' I answered reluctantly, because foolish tears were already welling up in my eyes. 'I woke up an hour before our meeting, but it was as if I hadn't slept. I don't know what was wrong with me. I was coming, so that I could tell you all this, as if time had stopped for me, as if a certain sensation, a certain feeling were going to remain with me forever from this time forward, as if a single minute would continue for a whole eternity and all life would come to a halt for me . . . When I woke up, it seemed to me that some sort of musical melody, long familiar, heard somewhere before, forgotten and sweet, was coming back to me. It seemed to me that all my life it had been begging to be released from my soul, and only now . . .'

'Ah, my goodness, my goodness!' Nastenka interrupted. 'What is all this about? I don't understand a single word.'

'Ah, Nastenka! I wanted somehow to convey this strange impression to you . . .' I began in a plaintive voice, which still harboured hope, albeit a very remote one.

'Enough, stop, enough!' she said, and in a single instant she figured out everything, the imp!

Suddenly she became somehow unusually talkative, gay and mischievous. She took me by the hand, laughing, she wanted me to laugh as well and each word of mine uttered in embarrassment was met with such ringing, such prolonged laughter . . . I began to get angry, she had suddenly started playing the coquette.

'Listen,' she began, 'I'm a bit disappointed, you know, that you didn't fall in love with me. Just try and understand human nature after that! But still and all, Mr Inflexible, you cannot but praise me for being such a simple girl. I tell you everything, everything, no matter what sort of foolishness comes into my head.'

'Listen! That's eleven o'clock, isn't it?' I said, when the measured sound of the bell began to ring in the distant city tower. She suddenly stopped, left off laughing and began to count.

'Yes, eleven,' she said at last in a timid, hesitant voice.

I at once regretted that I had frightened her, that I had made her count the hours, and I cursed myself for the fit of spite. I felt sorry for her and I didn't know how to atone for my transgression. I began to comfort her, to seek out reasons for his absence, to advance various arguments, proofs. Nobody could have been easier to deceive than she was at that moment, and indeed at such a time anyone would be happy to hear any sort of consolation whatsoever and is made ever so happy by even the shadow of an excuse.

'And the whole thing's ridiculous,' I began, becoming more and more excited, and admiring the unusual clarity of my own arguments, 'and he couldn't have come; you've misled me and bewitched me, Nastenka, so that I've lost track of the time . . . Now just think: he's only just got the letter; let's suppose that he can't come, let's suppose that he'll send an answer, then the letter couldn't come before tomorrow. I'll go as soon as it's light tomorrow and let you know at once. Consider, finally, that there are a thousand possibilities: well, he wasn't home when the letter arrived, and perhaps he still hasn't read it. You know, anything might have happened.'

'Yes, yes!' Nastenka answered, 'I didn't think of that; of course, anything might have happened,' she continued in her most compliant voice, in which, however, one could hear some other remote thought, like an annoying dissonance. 'Here's what you'll do,' she continued, 'you go as early as possible tomorrow and if you get anything, you'll let me know at once. You do know where I live, don't you?' And she began to repeat her address for me.

Then she suddenly became so tender, so timid with me . . . She seemed to be listening attentively to what I was saying to her; but when I addressed a question to her, she remained silent, got confused and turned her head away from me. I looked her in the eyes – I was right: she was crying.

'Now, how can you, how can you? Ah, you're such a child! What childishness! . . . Enough!'

She made an attempt to laugh, to calm herself, but her chin was trembling and her chest was still heaving.

'I was thinking about you,' she said to me after a minute's silence, 'you're so kind that I would have to be made of stone not to feel it. Do you know what just occurred to me? I was comparing the two of you. Why isn't he – you? Why isn't he like you? He's not as good as you, even though I love him more than you.'

I didn't say anything in reply. She seemed to be waiting for me to say something.

'Of course, perhaps I don't fully understand him yet, don't fully know him yet. You know, I was always a bit afraid of him; he was always so serious, he seemed so proud. Of course, I know that he only looks like that, that there is more tenderness in his heart than there is in mine . . . I remember how he looked at me then, when I, you remember, came to him with my bundle; but all the same I respect him too much, and doesn't that mean that we're not equals?'

'No, Nastenka, no,' I answered, 'that means that you love him more than anything in the world, and a good deal more than you love yourself.'

'Yes, I suppose that's so,' answered naive little Nastenka, 'but do you know what just occurred to me? Only I'm not going to talk about him now, but just in general; all of this occurred to me long ago. Listen, why is it that we aren't all like brothers to one another? Why is it that the very best person is always hiding something from other people and is quiet about it? Why not say frankly and immediately what's in your heart, if you know that you're not speaking idly? As it is, everyone looks more severe than they actually are, as though they're all afraid their feelings will be hurt if they reveal them too soon . . .'

'Ah, Nastenka! What you say is true; and, you see, there are many reasons for it,' I interrupted, reining in my feelings at that moment more than I had ever done before.

'No, no!' she answered with deep feeling. 'Now you, for example, aren't like other people! I really don't know how to tell you what I'm feeling; but it seems to me that you, for example . . . even now . . . it seems that you're sacrificing something for me,' she added timidly, with a fleeting glance at me. 'You'll forgive me for putting it like that: you see, I'm a simple girl; you see, I've seen very little of the world so far, and really at times I don't know how to talk,' she added in a voice that was trembling with some sort of hidden feeling, and meanwhile trying to smile, 'but I only wanted to tell you that I am grateful, that I feel all this as well . . . O, may God grant you happiness for this! Now then, everything that you told me then about your dreamer is absolutely untrue, that is, I wish to say that it doesn't have anything to do with you. You're getting better, you really are a completely different

65

person from the one you described. If you ever fall in love, then may God grant you happiness with her! But I won't wish her anything, because she will be happy with you. I know, I'm a woman myself, and you must believe me, when I tell you . . .'

She fell silent and firmly squeezed my hand. I couldn't say anything either because of the emotion. Several minutes passed.

'Yes, clearly he won't come today!' she said finally, raising her head. 'It's late! . . .'

'He'll come tomorrow,' I said in a most convincing and firm voice.

'Yes,' she added, having cheered up some, 'I now see myself that he won't come until tomorrow. Well then, goodbye! Until tomorrow! If it rains, then I might not come. But the day after tomorrow I'll come, I'll come without fail, no matter what; you be here without fail; I want to see you, I'll tell you everything.'

And later, as we were saying goodbye, she gave me her hand and said, looking at me brightly:

'You see, now we'll always be together, isn't that so?'

Oh, Nastenka, Nastenka! If only you knew how lonely I am now!

When it struck nine o'clock, I couldn't stay put in my room, I got dressed and went out, despite the foul weather. I was there, sitting on our bench. I started to walk down their lane, but I felt ashamed, and I turned back without having a look at their windows, when I was just a few steps away from their house. I came home more depressed than I had ever been. What a damp, boring time! If the weather had been fine, I would have walked about there all night long . . .

But until tomorrow! Until tomorrow! Tomorrow she will tell me everything.

However, there was no letter today. But that was to be expected. They're together by now . . .

THE FOURTH NIGHT

My God! How it has all come to an end! What an ending to all of this!

I arrived at nine o'clock. She was already there. I caught sight of her when I was still quite a distance away; she was standing like she had been then, that first time, with her elbows leaning on the railing of the embankment, and didn't hear me approach.

'Nastenka!' I called out to her, making a tremendous effort to suppress my agitation.

She quickly turned around towards me.

'Well!' she said, 'well, quickly now!'

I looked at her in bewilderment.

'Well, where's the letter? Did you bring the letter?' she repeated, clutching the railing with her hand.

'No, I don't have a letter,' I said finally, 'has he really not come to see you yet?'

She turned terribly pale and for a long time looked at me without moving. I had shattered her last hope.

'Well, good luck to him!' she uttered finally in a breaking voice. 'Good luck to him – if he's going to leave me like that.'

She lowered her eyes, then wanted to look at me, but

she couldn't. For several more minutes she kept her agitation in check, but suddenly she turned away, leaned her elbows on the balustrade of the embankment and burst into tears.

'Enough, enough!' I began, but as I looked at her I didn't have the strength to continue, and what could I have said?

'Don't try to comfort me,' she said, weeping, 'don't talk about him, don't say that he will come, that he wouldn't abandon me so cruelly, so inhumanly, as he has done. What for, what for? Can it really be that there was something in my letter, in that wretched letter? . . .'

Here her voice was broken by sobs; my heart was breaking as I looked at her.

'Oh, how cruelly inhuman it is!' she began again. 'And not a line, not a line! He could at least have answered that he didn't need me, that he was rejecting me; but not a single line in three whole days! How easy it is for him to wound, to insult a poor defenceless girl, whose only fault is that she loves him! Oh, what I've endured these three days! My God! My God! When I recall that I went to him the first time myself, that I humbled myself before him, wept, that I begged him for just the tiniest smidgen of love . . . And after that! . . . Listen,' she began, as she turned to me, and her black eyes began to flash, 'this cannot be! It simply cannot be like this; it's unnatural! Either you or I have been deceived; maybe he didn't get the letter? Perhaps he still doesn't know anything? How is it possible, judge for yourself, how is it possible to behave so barbarously and so coarsely as he has towards me! Not a single word! But the lowliest man on earth is treated with more compassion. Perhaps he heard something, perhaps somebody said something about me?' she cried out, turning to me with a question. 'What, what do you think?'

'Listen, Nastenka, tomorrow I'll go and see him in your name.'

'Yes?'

'I'll ask him about everything, I'll tell him everything.'

'Yes, yes?'

'You write a letter. Don't say no, Nastenka, don't say no! I'll make him respect your action, he'll learn everything, and if . . .'

'No, my friend, no,' she interrupted. 'Enough! Not another word, not another word from me, not a line, enough! I don't know him, I don't love him any more, I will for . . . get him . . .'

She didn't finish.

'Calm yourself, calm yourself! Sit here, Nastenka,' I said, as I seated her on the bench.

'But I am calm. Enough! It's nothing. Just tears, they'll dry! Do you think that I'll do away with myself, that I'll drown myself? . . .'

My heart was full; I wanted to say something, but couldn't.

'Listen!' she continued, taking me by the hand. 'Tell me, would you have acted like this? Would you have abandoned a girl who came to you on her own, would you have thrown in her face a shameless jeer at her weak, foolish heart? Would you have looked after her? Would you have understood that she was all alone, that she didn't know how to take care of herself, that she didn't know how to protect herself from loving you, that it wasn't her fault, that, finally, it wasn't her fault . . . that she had done nothing! . . . Oh, my God, my God! . . .'

'Nastenka,' I cried out finally, unable to control my agitation. 'Nastenka! You're tearing me apart! You're breaking my heart, you're killing me, Nastenka! I cannot be silent! I must finally speak, and tell you what has been welling up here, in my heart . . .'

As I said this, I got up from the bench. She took me by the hand and looked at me in surprise.

'What is it?' she uttered finally.

'Listen!' I said resolutely. 'Listen to me, Nastenka! What I am about to say is all nonsense, all impossible, all silly! I know that it can never happen, but I cannot remain silent. In the name of all that you are suffering now, I beg of you beforehand to forgive me! . . .'

'Well, what, what is it?' she said, having stopped crying and looking at me intently, while a strange curiosity shone in her astonished eyes. 'What is it?'

'It's impossible, but I love you, Nastenka! That's what it is! Well, now everything has been said!' I said with a wave of my hand. 'Now you will see whether you can talk with me as you were just talking, whether, finally, you can listen to what I'm going to say . . .'

'Well, what of it? What of it?' Nastenka interrupted, 'what of it? Well, I knew long ago that you loved me, only it always seemed to me that you loved me simply, in a different way . . . Oh, my God, my God!'

'In the beginning it was simple, Nastenka, but now, now . . . I'm in exactly the same position as you were when you went to him with your bundle. Worse than you, Nastenka, because he didn't love someone then, but you do.'

'What is it you're saying to me! I truly don't understand you at all. But listen here, why ever, that is, not why, but what reason do you have for so suddenly . . . My God! I'm talking nonsense! But you . . .'

And Nastenka became thoroughly confused. Her cheeks were flushed; she lowered her eyes.

'What's to be done, Nastenka, what am I to do? I am to blame, I abused your . . . But no, no, I'm not to blame, Nastenka; I know it, I feel it, because my heart tells me that I'm right, because I cannot hurt you, I cannot offend you! I was your friend; well, and that is what I am now; I have betrayed nothing. You see, now it's me whose tears are streaming down, Nastenka. Let them stream, let them stream – they won't bother anybody. They will dry, Nastenka . . .'

'But sit down, do sit down,' she said, as she was seating me on the bench, 'oh, my God!'

'No, Nastenka, I won't sit down; I can't stay here any longer, you won't see me any more; I'll say everything and leave. I only want to say that you would never have learned that I love you. I would have buried my secret. I would not have tormented you, at this moment, with my egoism. No! But I couldn't bear it any longer now; you spoke of it yourself, you are to blame, you are to blame for all this, not me. You can't drive me away from you . . .'

'No, of course not, no, I'm not driving you off, no!' Nastenka said, concealing, as best she could, her embarrassment, the poor thing.

'You're not driving me away? No! But I was going to run away from you myself. And I will leave, as soon as I tell you everything from the beginning, because when you were talking just now, I couldn't sit still, when you were crying just now, when you were suffering because, well because (I'll say it, Nastenka), because you were rejected, because your love had been spurned, I sensed, I felt in my heart that there was so much love for you, Nastenka, so much love! . . . And I was so sorry that I couldn't help you with this love . . . that my heart was breaking, and I, I – could not be silent, I had to speak, Nastenka, I had to speak! . . .'

'Yes, yes! Speak to me, speak to me like that!' Nastenka said with an inexplicable gesture. 'It might seem strange to you that I'm speaking to you like this, but . . . speak! I'll tell you later! I'll tell you everything!'

'You feel sorry for me, Nastenka; you simply feel sorry for me, my little friend! What's done is done! What's said can't be taken back! Isn't that so? Well, now you know everything. Well, that's a starting point. Well, all right! Everything's fine now; only listen. When you were sitting and crying, I was thinking to myself (oh, let me tell you what I was thinking!), I was thinking that (well, of course, this could never be, Nastenka), I was thinking that you . . . I was thinking that you somehow . . . well, that you quite on your own had stopped loving him. Then – I was thinking this yesterday and the day before yesterday, Nastenka – then I would have made you, I would certainly have made you fall in love with me; you said, you know, you were saying yourself, Nastenka, that you had almost fallen in love with me. Well, what else? Well, that's almost everything that I wanted to say; it remains only to say what it would have been like if you had fallen in love with me, only that, nothing more! Listen then, my friend – because you are still my friend – of course, I'm a simple person, poor and insignificant, only that's not the point (I somehow keep talking about the wrong things, that's because I'm embarrassed, Nastenka), but only I would love you so, I would love you so, that even if you still loved him and continued to love this person whom I don't know, you still would not find my love to be a burden to you in any way. You would only feel, you would only sense at every moment that next to you beats a grateful, grateful heart, an ardent heart, which for your sake . . . Oh, Nastenka, Nastenka! What have you done to me! . . .'

'Now, don't cry, I don't want you to cry,' Nastenka said, quickly getting up from the bench, 'come along, get up, come with me, don't cry, don't cry,' she kept saying, as she wiped away my tears with her handkerchief, 'well, come along now; perhaps I'll tell you something . . . Yes, if he has abandoned me now, if he has forgotten me, even though I still love him (I don't wish to deceive you) . . . but, listen, answer me. If, for example, I were to love you, that is, if only I . . . Oh, my friend, my friend! When I think, when I think how I insulted you then when I laughed at your love, when I praised you for not falling in love! . . . Oh, my God! How did I not foresee it, how did I not foresee this, how could I have been so stupid, but . . . Well, well, I've made up my mind, I'll tell you everything . . .'

'Listen, Nastenka, do you know what? I'll go away, that's what! I'm simply tormenting you. Now you have pangs of remorse because you made fun of me, but I don't want, yes, I don't want you, in addition to your sorrow . . . Of course, I'm to blame, Nastenka, but goodbye!'

'Stop, hear me out: can you wait?'

'Wait for what, why?'

'I love him; but that will pass, it must pass, it cannot but pass; it's already passing, I can sense it . . . Who knows, perhaps it will even end today, because I hate him, because he's had a good laugh at my expense, while you were crying here with me, because you didn't reject me, like he did, because you love me, and he didn't love me, because finally I love you myself . . . yes, I love! I love as you love me; you know, I myself even said so to you, you heard it yourself – because I love that you are better than he is, because you are nobler than he is, because, because he . . .'

The poor girl's agitation was so intense that she didn't finish, she put her head on my shoulder, then on my chest and burst into bitter tears. I comforted her, tried to bring her round, but she couldn't stop; she kept squeezing my hand and saying between sobs: 'Wait, wait, I'll stop in just a minute! I want to tell you . . . don't think that these tears – it's just weakness, wait until it passes . . .' Finally, she stopped, wiped away her tears and we set off walking once again. I wanted to speak, but for a long time yet she kept asking me to wait. We fell silent . . . Finally, she plucked up her courage and began to speak.

'Now listen to me,' she began in a weak and trembling voice, but one in which there was a ring of something that pierced right through my heart and began to ache there sweetly, 'don't think that I am so fickle and flighty, don't think that I can so easily and quickly forget and be untrue . . . I loved him for a whole year and I swear to God that never, never was I unfaithful to him even in thought. He disdained this; he had a good laugh at my expense – good luck to him! But he wounded me and insulted my heart. I – I do not love him, because I can love only that which is magnanimous, which understands me, which is noble; because I am like that myself, and he is not worthy of me – well, good luck to him! It's better that he disappoint me now than for me to learn what he's like later on . . . Well, of course! But who knows, my dear friend,' she continued, squeezing my hand, 'who knows, perhaps all my love amounted to nothing more than my feelings and imagination, just my imagination, perhaps it began as a prank or foolishness, all because I was under Grandmother's watch. Perhaps I ought to love someone else, another, and not him, not a man like him, but someone who would take pity on me, and, and . . . Well, let's leave it at that, let's leave it at that,' Nastenka broke off, choked with emotion, 'I only wanted to say to you . . . I wanted to say that if, despite the fact that I love him (no, loved him), if, despite that, you will still say . . . if you feel that your love is so great that it may in the end drive out from my heart the former . . . if you wish to take pity on me, if you don't wish to leave me alone to my fate, without consolation, without hope, if you wish to love me always as you now love me, then I swear that gratitude . . . that my love will in the end be worthy of your love . . . Will you take my hand now?'

'Nastenka,' I cried out, choking with sobs, 'Nastenka! . . . Oh, Nastenka! . . .'

'Well, enough, enough! Well, now that's certainly enough!' she said, hardly able to control herself, 'well, now everything has been said; isn't that right? Isn't that so? Well, and you're happy, and I'm happy; not another word more about this; wait – spare me . . . Talk about something else, for God's sake! . . .'

'Yes, Nastenka, yes! Enough about that, now I am happy, I . . . Well, Nastenka, well, let's talk about something else, quickly; yes, quickly, let's talk about something else; yes! I'm ready . . .'

And we didn't know what to say, we laughed, we cried, we said thousands of words without rhyme or reason; we first walked along the sidewalk, then suddenly we turned back and crossed the street; then we stopped and began to cross over to the embankment; we were like children . . .

'I live alone now, Nastenka,' I said, 'but tomorrow . . . Well, of course, I'm poor, you know, Nastenka, I only have twelve hundred roubles, but that doesn't matter . . .'

'Of course not, and Grandmother has her pension; so she won't be a burden to us. We must take Grandmother.'

'Of course, we must take Grandmother . . . Only there's Matryona . . .'

'Oh, and we have Fyokla as well!'

'Matryona is a good woman, only she has one fault: she doesn't have any imagination, Nastenka, absolutely no imagination whatsoever; but that doesn't matter! . . .'

'It doesn't make any difference; they can both live together; only you must move to our house tomorrow.'

'What did you say? To your house? Fine, I'm ready . . .'

'Yes, you'll rent from us. We have an attic upstairs, it's empty; there was a lodger, an old woman, a noblewoman, she's moved out, and Grandmother, I know, wants to rent it to a young man; I said: "Why exactly a young man?" And she says: "Just because, I'm old now, but just don't you start thinking, Nastenka, that I want to marry you off to him." So I guessed that it was for that very reason . . .'

'Oh, Nastenka! . . .'

And we both laughed.

'Well, enough of that, enough. But where is it that you live? I've forgotten.'

'Over there, by —sky Bridge, in Barannikov's building.'

'Is it that big house?'

'Yes, the big house.'

'Oh, I know it, it's a good house; only you must leave it, you know, and move in with us as soon as possible . . .'

'Tomorrow, then, Nastenka, tomorrow; I owe a bit for my apartment, but that doesn't matter . . . I'll receive my salary soon . . .'

'And you know, perhaps I can give lessons; I'll learn something myself and then I'll give lessons . . .'

'Well, now that's wonderful . . . and I'll get my bonus soon, Nastenka . . .'

'So, then, tomorrow you'll be my lodger . . .'

'Yes, and we'll go see *The Barber of Seville*, because they're going to put it on again soon.'

'Yes, let's go,' Nastenka said, smiling, 'no, it would be better to see something else and not the *Barber* . . .'

'Well, fine, something else; of course, that would be better, what was I thinking . . .'

As we said this, we were both walking in some kind of stupor, in a haze, as if we didn't know ourselves what was happening to us. One moment we would stop and talk for a long time without moving, then we would start walking again and God only knows where we ended up, and then laughter again, and then tears . . . Then Nastenka would suddenly want to go home, and I didn't dare keep her and wanted to see her home; we would set off and a quarter of an hour later we would find ourselves on the embankment by our bench. Then she would sigh, and once again her eyes would well up with tears; I would turn timid, and then feel a chill . . . But she would immediately squeeze my hand and drag me off to walk, to chatter, to talk . . .

'It's time now, it's time for me to go home; I think it must be quite late,' Nastenka said at last, 'we've been behaving like children long enough!'

'Yes, Nastenka, only I won't fall asleep now; I won't go home.'

'I don't think I'll sleep either; just see me home . . .'

'Absolutely!'

'Only this time we absolutely must walk all the way to the apartment.'

'Absolutely, absolutely . . .'

'Word of honour? . . . Because, you see, I must return home at some point!'

'Word of honour,' I answered, laughing . . .

'Well, let's go!'

'Let's go! Look at the sky, Nastenka, look! Tomorrow will be a wonderful day; what a blue sky, what a moon! Look: see how that yellow cloud is beginning to hide it from view, look, look! . . . No, it's passed by. Look now, look! . . .'

But Nastenka wasn't looking at the cloud, she stood speechless, rooted to the ground; a minute later she began somewhat timidly clinging to me tightly. Her hand began to tremble in my hand; I glanced at her . . . She pressed against me more tightly still . . .

At that moment a young man walked past us. He suddenly stopped, looked at us intently and then took several steps. My heart began to quiver . . .

'Nastenka,' I said in a hushed voice, 'who is that, Nastenka?'

'It's him!' she answered in a whisper, clinging to me even more tightly and more timidly . . . I could barely keep standing on my own two feet.

'Nastenka! Nastenka! It's you!' we heard a voice behind us, and at that moment the young man took several steps towards us.

My God, what a cry! How she shuddered! How she tore herself from my arms and flew to meet him! ... I stood and watched them, crushed. But she had scarcely given him her hand, had scarcely thrown herself into his embrace, when she suddenly turned to me again, and was at my side in a flash, like the wind, and before I had a chance to collect myself, she flung both arms around my neck and kissed me firmly, ardently. Then, without saying a word to me, she rushed to him again, took him by the hand and led him away.

I stood for a long time and watched them walk away ... Finally, both of them vanished from sight.

MORNING

My nights ended with the morning. It was a dreadful day. The rain beat down on my windows cheerlessly; it was dark in the room, it was overcast outside. My head ached and was spinning; fever was stealing its way through my limbs.

'A letter for you, sir, it came by the city post, the postman brought it,' Matryona said, hovering over me.

'A letter! From whom?' I cried out, jumping up from my chair.

'That I wouldn't know, sir, have a look; maybe it's written down there who it's from.'

I broke the seal. It was from her!

Oh, forgive, forgive me! (Nastenka wrote me) I beg you on my knees to forgive me! I deceived both you and myself. It was a dream, a phantom . . . I have suffered torments about you today; forgive me, forgive me! . . .

Don't blame me, because I haven't changed in the least towards you; I said that I would love you, and I love you now, I more than love you. Oh, my God! If only I could love you both at the same time! Oh, if only you were he!

'Oh, if only he were you!' flashed through my mind. I remembered your words, Nastenka!

God knows what I would do for you now! I know that you're miserable and sad. I have hurt you, but you know – when one loves, an injury is soon forgotten. And you love me!

Thank you! Yes, thank you for that love! Because it is stamped on my memory like a sweet dream that you remember long after waking up; because I will forever remember that moment when you opened up your heart to me like a brother and so generously accepted the gift of my shattered heart to protect, cherish and heal it . . . If you forgive me, then the memory of you will be exalted in me by a feeling of eternal gratitude to you that will never quit my heart . . . I will keep that memory alive, I will be true to it, I will not betray it, I will not betray my heart: it is too constant. It returned so quickly yesterday to him to whom it had always belonged.

We will meet, you will visit us, you will not abandon us, you will always be a friend, my brother . . . And when you see me, you will give me your hand . . . won't you? You will give it to me, you have forgiven me, isn't that so? Do you love me as you did *before*?

Oh, love me, don't leave me, because I love you so at this moment, because I am worthy of your love, because I will deserve it . . . my dear friend! Next week I am to be married to him. He returned in love with me, he never forgot me . . . You won't be angry that I have written about him. But I want to come and see you with him; you will love him, won't you? . . .

Forgive me, remember and love your –

Nastenka

I read that letter over and over again for a long time; the tears welled up in my eyes. At last it fell out of my hands, and I covered my face with my hands.

'Dearie! Come now, dearie!' Matryona began.

'What is it, old woman?'

'I got all the cobwebs off the ceiling; now you can get married, or invite some guests, it's just the time for it . . .'

I looked at Matryona . . . She was still a hale and hearty, *young* old woman, but I don't know why, suddenly I pictured her with a vacant stare, wrinkled face, stooped, decrepit. I don't know why but I suddenly pictured that my room had aged as much as the old woman. The walls and floors were faded, everything had become dingy; and the cobwebs had multiplied so there were more than ever before. I don't know why, when I glanced out the window, it seemed to me that the house opposite had also become decrepit and dingy, that the plasterwork on the columns was peeling and crumbling, that the cornices had turned black and were cracked, and that the walls which had been painted a bright, deep yellow had become patchy . . .

Either a ray of sunshine, after suddenly peeping out

from behind a cloud, had again hidden behind a rain cloud, and everything had darkened again before my eyes; or perhaps the whole vista of my future had flashed before me so bleakly and so sadly, and I saw myself just as I am now exactly fifteen years later, only older, in the same room, just as lonely, with the same Matryona, who hasn't grown any wiser in all those years.

But that I should nurse a grudge, Nastenka! That I should cast a dark cloud over your bright, serene happiness; that I, with bitter reproaches, should cast pangs of anguish on your heart, wound it with secret remorse and force it to beat with anguish at the moment of bliss; that I would crush even one of those delicate flowers that you plaited into your black curls when you walked together with him to the altar . . . Oh, never, never! May your sky be clear, may your sweet smile be bright and serene, may you be blessed for that moment of bliss and happiness that you gave to another lonely, grateful heart!

My God! A whole minute of bliss! Is that really so little for the whole of a man's life?

1848

Bobok

This time I'm submitting 'The Notes of a Certain Person'. It is not I; it is by an altogether different person. I think nothing more in the way of an introduction is necessary.

THE NOTES OF A CERTAIN PERSON

The day before yesterday Semyon Ardalyonovich suddenly comes out with:

'And would you kindly tell me, Ivan Ivanych, will the day come when you'll be sober?'

A strange request. I don't take offence, I'm a shy person; but, just the same, they've gone and made me out to be a madman. An artist happened to paint my portrait: 'After all,' he says, 'you're a literary man.' I acquiesced, and he exhibited it. I read: 'Go take a look at this sickly face that is on the verge of madness.'

Even if my face is like that, really how can one be so direct in print? In print everything should be noble: there should be ideals, but here . . .

At the very least say it indirectly, that's what you have style for. No, he doesn't want to do it indirectly. Nowadays humour and good style are disappearing and swear words are taken for wit. I'm not offended, I'm not some God-knows-what-kind of fancy man of letters to lose my mind over something like that. I wrote a story – it wasn't published. I wrote a feuilleton – it was rejected. I took a lot of these feuilletons around to different publishers, and was rejected everywhere: 'You don't have enough salt,' they told me.

'What kind of salt do you want?' I ask with scorn. 'Attic salt?'

He doesn't even understand. For the most part, I translate from French for the booksellers. And I write advertisements for the merchants. 'A rare treat! Fine tea,' I write, 'from our own plantations . . .' I made a bundle on a panegyric for His Excellency, the late Pyotr Matveyevich. I was commissioned by a bookseller to compile *The Art of Pleasing the Ladies*. I've put out about six books like this in my lifetime. I want to collect Voltaire's *bon mots*, but I'm afraid that they'll seem a bit flat to people here. Who needs Voltaire now; these days it's a cudgel you need, not Voltaire! We've knocked out each other's teeth – every last one! Well, and that's the whole extent of my literary endeavours. Although I do dispatch letters to the editorial offices free of charge, signed with my name in full. I give advice and make recommendations, I offer criticism and point out the proper path. Last week I sent my fortieth letter in two years to a certain editorial office; I've spent four roubles on stamps alone. I have a nasty temper, that's what it is.

I think the painter did my portrait not for the sake of literature, but for the sake of the two symmetrical warts on my forehead: it's a phenomenon, he says. They don't have any ideas, so now they resort to phenomena. Well, and what a fine job he did of capturing my warts in the portrait – they're lifelike! That's what they call realism.

And as far as madness is concerned, last year a lot of people were put down as mad. And with such style: 'Such an original talent . . .' they say, 'and then towards the end it turned out that . . . However, this should have been foreseen long ago . . .' This is still rather ingenious; so that one might even praise it from the point of view of pure art. Well, and then suddenly these madmen came back even smarter. There you are – we know how to drive people out of their minds, but we've never made anyone smarter . . .

In my opinion, the one who's smarter than all the rest is the one who calls himself a fool at least once a month – an unheard of talent nowadays! Before, a fool knew once a year at the very least that he was a fool, but now nothing doing. And they've muddled things so that you can't tell a fool from an intelligent person. They do this on purpose.

I'm reminded of a Spanish witticism, when two and a half centuries ago the French built the first madhouse:

'They locked up all their fools in a special building to reassure themselves that they're the sane ones.' But really, locking somebody else up in a madhouse doesn't prove that you have brains. 'K. lost his mind, that means that we are sane.' No, that isn't what that means.

However, what the devil . . . and why am I fussing about my brains: I grumble and grumble. Even the servant girl is tired of it. Yesterday a friend dropped by: 'Your style is changing,' he says, 'it's choppy. You chop and chop – and then you've got a parenthetic clause, then you pile on another parenthetic clause, and then you stick something else in parentheses, and then you start chopping and chopping again . . .'

My friend's right. Something strange is happening to me. And my character is changing, and my head aches. I'm beginning to see and hear certain strange things. Not exactly voices, but it's as if someone were right beside me, saying: '*Bobok, bobok, bobok!*'

What is this *bobok*? I need some diversion.

I went out in search of diversion and ended up at a funeral. A distant relative. A collegiate councillor, however. A widow, five daughters, all young. What it must come to just for shoes alone! The deceased managed, but now there's only a little pension. They'll have their tails between their legs. I had always been given a less than hearty welcome. And I wouldn't have gone now if it hadn't been such a special occasion. I took part in the procession to the cemetery along with the others; they keep their distance and put on airs. My uniform, indeed, is in pretty bad shape. It's been about twenty-five years, I think, since I've been to the cemetery; there's a nice little place for you!

First of all, the smell. About fifteen corpses had arrived. Palls of various prices; there were even two catafalques: one for a general and one for some lady. There were a lot of mournful faces, and a lot of bogus mourning as well, and even a lot of undisguised gaiety. The clergy can't complain: it's money. But the smell, the smell. I wouldn't want to be one of the local ecclesiastics.

I took a cautious look at the corpses, not having confidence in controlling my impressionability. There were some gentle expressions, but there were unpleasant ones as well. Generally, the smiles weren't very nice, and some were quite far from nice. I don't like them; I'll have dreams about them.

During the service I walked out of the church for some air; it was a greyish day, but dry. It was cold as well; well, it is October after all. I walked for a bit among the graves. There are various classes. The third class costs thirty roubles: decent and not too expensive. The first two classes are inside the church and under the church porch; well, they charge an arm and a leg for those. This time there were six third-class burials, including the general and the lady.

I glanced in the graves – it was terrible: water, and

what water! It was absolutely green and . . . well, let's leave it at that! The gravedigger was constantly bailing it out with a bucket. As the service was still going on, I strolled outside the gates. There's an almshouse right there and a bit further on there's a restaurant. The little restaurant wasn't bad – fair to middling – and you can get a bite to eat and everything. It was packed with mourners. I noticed a good deal of merrymaking and heartfelt liveliness. I had a bite to eat and something to drink.

Later I took part with my own hands in bearing the coffin from the church to the grave. Why is it that corpses are so heavy in their coffins? They say that it's because of some sort of inertia, that the body is no longer in control of itself . . . or some such nonsense; it contradicts mechanics and common sense. I don't like it when people with only a general education rush in to solve problems best left to specialists; and that happens all the time among us. Civilians like to have opinions on military matters, even those that concern a field marshal, while people educated as engineers more often than not have opinions on philosophy and political economy.

I didn't go to the prayer service. I'm proud, and if I'm only to be received out of dire necessity, then why should I trail along to their dinners, even if it is a funeral dinner? Only I don't understand why I stayed on at the cemetery; I sat down on a monument and became suitably thoughtful.

I began with the Moscow exhibition and ended with the subject of astonishment in general. Here's what I came up with about 'astonishment':

'To be astonished at everything, of course, is silly, while to be astonished at nothing is much more handsome, and for some reason is recognized as good form. But surely it's not like that in reality. In my opinion, it's much sillier to be astonished at nothing than to be astonished at everything. And what's more: to be astonished at nothing is almost the same thing as to respect nothing. And a silly man is not capable of showing respect.'

'And above all I want to feel respect. I *thirst* to feel respect,' an acquaintance of mine said to me on one occasion recently.

He thirsts to feel respect! And my God, I thought, what would become of you if you dared to print that now!

And that's when I started daydreaming. I don't like reading the inscriptions on gravestones; it's forever the same thing. A half-eaten sandwich lay on the gravestone next to me: it was silly and out of place. I threw it on the ground, since it wasn't bread but just a sandwich. However, dropping bread crumbs on the ground isn't a sin, it seems; it's when it's on the floor that it's a sin. I should look it up in Suvorin's calendar.

One might suppose that I'd been sitting there for a long time, even too long; that is, I even lay down on a long stone in the shape of a marble coffin. And how did it happen that I suddenly began to hear various things? At first

93

I didn't pay any attention and regarded it with disdain. However, the conversation continued. I listened – the sounds were muffled, as though they had pillows covering their mouths; and yet they were intelligible and very near. I roused myself, sat up and began to listen carefully.

'Your Excellency, this is simply impossible, sir. You declared hearts, I'm following your lead and suddenly you have the seven of diamonds. We should have made arrangements about diamonds earlier, sir.'

'What's that, you mean we should play by rote? Where's the attraction in that?'

'You can't, Your Excellency. You can't play without rules. We absolutely must have a dummy and the cards must be dealt face down.'

'Well, you won't find a dummy here.'

What arrogant words, however! Both strange and unexpected. One voice was so weighty and dignified, while the other seemed softly honeyed; I wouldn't have believed it if I hadn't heard it myself. I didn't think I was at the prayer service. And yet how was it that they're playing preference here and who was this general? That it was coming from under the gravestone there could be no doubt. I bent down and read the inscription on the tombstone.

'Here lies the body of Major General Pervoyedov . . . Knight of such and such orders.' Hm. 'Passed away in August of the year . . . fifty-seven . . . Rest, dear ashes, until the joyful morn!'

Hm, the devil, he really is a general! There wasn't a tombstone yet on the other grave, the one the ingratiating voice came from; there was only a stone slab; must be a newcomer. Judging by his voice he was a court councillor.

'Oh-ho-ho-ho!' an altogether different voice could be heard coming from a quite new grave some dozen yards away from the general's spot. It belonged to a man of the common people, but modulated to an obsequiously pious manner.

'Oh-ho-ho-ho!'

'Ah, he's hiccuping again!' suddenly resounded the squeamish and haughty voice of an irritated lady, who seemed to be from the highest society. 'My punishment is to lie next to this shopkeeper!'

'No, I didn't hiccup at all, and I haven't taken any food, it's simply my nature. And still and all, my lady, these whims of yours just won't let you settle down here.'

'So why did you have to lie down here?'

'They put me here, my wife and the little ones put me here, I didn't lie down here myself. The mysteries of death! And I wouldn't have lain down next to you for anything, not for all the money in the world; but my own capital got me my place here, reckoning by the price, madam. For we can always do that, I mean, put enough aside for our own third-class grave.'

'You made a bundle, cheated people?'

'How could we cheat you, when it seems there's been

no payment from you since January? We've got a little bill in your name at the shop.'

'Well, now that's silly; in my opinion, it's very silly to look to have debts settled here! Go upstairs. Ask my niece; she's my heir.'

'But who can I ask now and where can I go? We have both reached the end, and before the judgement seat of God we are equal in our trespasses.'

'In our trespasses!' the dead woman mimicked disdainfully. 'And don't you dare speak another word to me!'

'Oh-ho-ho-ho!'

'The shopkeeper nevertheless obeys the lady, Your Excellency.'

'And why shouldn't he obey?'

'Well, Your Excellency, as we know there's a new order here.'

'What new order is that?'

'Well, you see, we're dead, so to speak, Your Excellency.'

'Ah, yes! But still there's order . . .'

Well, haven't they done us a favour! What a comfort! If it's already reached this point here, then why bother questioning what it's like upstairs? But how they carry on! However, I continued listening, though with extreme indignation.

'No, I would have lived a bit longer! No . . . I, you know . . . I would have lived a bit!' a new voice suddenly made itself heard from somewhere between the general and the irritable lady.

'Do you hear, Your Excellency, our friend is at it again. He's quiet as can be for three days, and then suddenly: "I would have lived a bit! yes, I would have lived a bit!" And, you know, with such an appetite, he-he!'

'And with such thoughtlessness.'

'He can't help it, Your Excellency, and, you know, he falls asleep, he's already fast asleep; after all he's been here since April, you see, and then suddenly: "I would have lived a bit."'

'On the boring side, though,' His Excellency observed.

'On the boring side, Your Excellency. Perhaps we should tease Avdotya Ignatyevna again, he-he?'

'Please don't, spare me that. I can't stand that quick-tempered crybaby.'

'And I, for that matter, can't stand the two of you either,' the crybaby answered contemptuously. 'You're both incredible bores and you don't know how to talk about the ideal. I know a little story about you, Your Excellency – don't flatter yourself – about how a servant swept you out with a broom from under a certain married couple's bed one morning.'

'Nasty woman!' the general muttered through clenched teeth.

'Dear Avdotya Ignatyevna,' the shopkeeper cried out again suddenly, 'my dear lady, tell me, and don't hold it against me, am I in the torments now, or is something else happening?'

'Ah, he's back on the same thing again; I had a feeling he would be, because there's a smell coming from him, a smell from his tossing and turning.'

'I'm not tossing and turning, ma'am, and there's no particular smell coming from me, because I've still managed to preserve my body whole, while you, my lady, have really started to go bad – because the smell indeed is unbearable, even for this place. I've kept quiet merely out of politeness.'

'Ah, you and your nasty insults! He's the one who reeks, and he blames me.'

'Oh-ho-ho-ho! If only these forty days would pass: I'd hear tearful voices above me, my wife wailing and the children softly weeping! . . .'

'Well, what a thing to weep about: they'll stuff themselves with *kutya* and leave. Ah, if only somebody would wake up!'

'Avdotya Ignatyevna,' the smooth-tongued official spoke up, 'wait a little bit, the new ones will start talking.'

'And are there any young people among them?'

'Young people as well, Avdotya Ignatyevna. There are even some young men.'

'Ah, just what we need!'

'What, haven't they begun yet?' His Excellency enquired.

'Even the ones from the day before yesterday haven't woken up yet, Your Excellency, you yourself know that sometimes they're quiet for a week. It's a good thing that yesterday and the day before and today they brought a whole lot all at once. Otherwise, you see, they're all from last year for seventy feet around.'

'Yes, that should be interesting.'

'Now, Your Excellency, today they buried Tarasevich, the actual privy councillor. I recognized the voices. I know his nephew who helped lower the coffin just now.'

'Hm, whereabout is he then?'

'About five paces away from you, Your Excellency, to the left. He's almost at your feet, sir . . . There's somebody you should get acquainted with, Your Excellency.'

'Hm, no . . . I shouldn't be the first to make a move.'

'But he'll do that, Your Excellency. He'll even be flattered; leave it to me, Your Excellency, and I'll . . .'

'Ah, ah . . . Ah, what's happening to me?' somebody's frightened, new little voice suddenly wheezed.

'It's a new one, Your Excellency, a new one, thank God, and so soon! Sometimes they're silent for a whole week.'

'Ah, I believe it's a young man!' Avdotya Ignatyevna cried out.

'I . . . I . . . I . . . from complications, and so suddenly!' the youth began to babble again. 'Just the day before Schultz tells me: "You have complications," he says, and suddenly I up and die by the morning. Ah! Ah!'

'Well, there's nothing to be done, young man,' observed

the general kindly, evidently delighted by the novice. 'You must console yourself. Welcome to our Vale of Jehoshaphat, so to speak. We're good people, you'll get to know us and appreciate us. Major General Vasily Vasilyev Pervoyedov, at your service.'

'Ah, no! No, no, absolutely not, sir! I went to Schultz; you see, I had complications, first in my chest and then a cough, and later I caught cold: the chest and the flu . . . and then suddenly, quite unexpectedly . . . that's the main thing, it was quite unexpected.'

'You say that it started in the chest,' the official gently interjected, as if wishing to encourage the novice.

'Yes, the chest and phlegm, but then suddenly the phlegm and chest were gone, and I couldn't breathe . . . and you know . . .'

'I know, I know. But if it was the chest, you should have gone to Ecke, not to Schultz.'

'But, you know, I kept meaning to go to Botkin . . . and suddenly . . .'

'Well, but Botkin's unreasonable,' the general observed.

'Ah, no, he's not at all unreasonable; I've heard that he's so attentive and will tell you everything in advance.'

'His Excellency was referring to the price,' the official set him straight.

'Ah, not at all, just three roubles, and he examines you so well, and you get a prescription . . . and I definitely wanted to, because I was told . . . So then, gentlemen, should I go see Ecke or Botkin?'

'What? See whom?' the general's corpse began to rock with pleasant laughter. The official followed suit in falsetto.

'Dear boy, dear, delightful boy, how I love you!' Avdotya Ignatyevna cried out, beside herself. 'Now if only they'd put one like you next to me!'

No, I simply cannot countenance that! And this is the dead of today! However, I should listen some more and not jump to conclusions. This whimpering novice – I remember seeing him in his coffin earlier – wore the expression of a frightened chicken, the most revolting thing in the whole world! However, what's next?

But what came next was such a muddled affair that I didn't manage to retain all of it in my memory, for a great many of them woke up all at once: an official woke up, a state councillor, and he began immediately discussing with the general the project of a new subcommittee in the Department of — Affairs and in connection with this about the probable transfer of public servants, all of which the general found very, very entertaining. I confess that I also learned a lot that was new, so much so that I marvelled at the ways by which it is sometimes possible to come by government news in this capital. Then an engineer half woke up, but for a long time afterwards muttered such absolute nonsense that our friends didn't bother him, but instead let him rest. Finally, the noble lady who had been buried under the catafalque that

morning showed signs of sepulchral animation. Lebezyatnikov (for the ingratiating court councillor whom I
detested turned out to be named Lebezyatnikov) was
surprised and made a great deal of fuss that they were
all waking up so soon this time. I confess, I was surprised
as well; however, some of those who woke up had been
buried the day before yesterday, for example, a very
young girl, about sixteen years old, but who was all
giggles . . . disgusting and lustful giggles.

'Your Excellency, Privy Counsillor Tarasevich is
waking up!' Lebezyatnikov suddenly announced with
extraordinary urgency.

'Eh? What's that?' the suddenly awakened privy councillor mumbled demandingly in a lisping voice. His voice
sounded both capricious and imperious. I listened with
curiosity, for during these past few days I had heard
something about this Tarasevich – something highly
suggestive and alarming.

'It's me, Your Excellency, sir, so far it's only me, sir.'

'What do you want and how can I help you?'

'Merely to enquire after Your Excellency's health; not
being accustomed to the circumstances here, sir, everybody at first feels rather cramped, as it were . . . General
Pervoyedov would like to have the honour of making
Your Excellency's acquaintance and wishes . . .'

'Never heard of him.'

'For goodness' sake, Your Excellency, General Pervoyedov, Vasily Vasilyevich . . .'

'Are you General Pervoyedov?'

'No, Your Excellency, I am merely Court Councillor Lebezyatnikov, sir, at your service, but General Pervoyedov . . .'

'Nonsense! And I'll ask you to leave me in peace.'

'Let him be,' General Pervoyedov himself, with a dignified air, finally put a stop to the vile haste of his sepulchral attendant.

'He's not fully awake yet, Your Excellency, you need to take that into consideration, sir; it's on account that he's not accustomed, sir: he'll wake up and then he'll take it differently, sir . . .'

'Let him be,' the general repeated.

'Vasily Vasilyevich! Hey you, Your Excellency!' an entirely new voice suddenly cried out loudly and excitedly, right next to Avdotya Ignatyevna. It was the impertinent voice of a gentleman with a fashionably weary mode of expression and impudent delivery. 'I've been observing all of you for two hours now; I've been lying here three days now; do you remember me, Vasily Vasilyevich? Klinevich, we used to meet at the Volokonskys, where, I don't know why, you were also received.'

'What, Count Pyotr Petrovich . . . is that really you? . . . and at such a young age . . . I am so sorry!'

'And I'm sorry myself, but it's really all the same to me, and I want to get as much as possible from every quarter here. And it's not Count, but Baron, I'm merely a baron.

We're some sort of mangy little barons, our people were lackeys, and I don't know why – to hell with it! I'm merely a scoundrel from pseudo-high society and thought to be a charming *polisson*. My father was some sort of little general, and my mother was once received *en haut lieu*. Zieffel the Yid and I passed off 50,000 roubles in counterfeit banknotes, and I informed against him, but Yulka Charpentier de Lusignan carried off all the money with her to Bordeaux. And, just imagine, my engagement had already been announced – to Shchevalevskaya, just three months shy of sixteen, still in school, with a dowry of 90,000. Avdotya Ignatyevna, do you remember how you corrupted me, fifteen years ago, when I was still a fourteen-year-old page? . . .'

'Ah, so it's you, you scoundrel; well, at least God sent you, because otherwise here it's . . .'

'You were wrong to suspect your merchant neighbour of smelling bad . . . I just kept quiet and laughed. You see, it's me; they buried me in a nailed coffin.'

'Ugh, you're disgusting! But I'm glad all the same; you wouldn't believe, Klinevich, you wouldn't believe how scarce life and wit are here.'

'Yes, I know, yes, I know, and I'm determined to get something original going here. Your Excellency – not you, Pervoyedov – the other one, Mr Tarasevich, the privy councillor! Answer me! It's Klinevich, I'm the one who took you to see Mlle Furie during Lent. Can you hear me?'

'I hear you, Klinevich, and I'm very glad, and believe me . . .'

'I don't believe you for a minute and don't give a damn! I simply want to kiss you, you dear old thing, and thank God I can't. Do you know, gentlemen, the trick that this *grand-père* came up with? He died two or three days ago and, can you imagine, he left behind a shortfall of a total of 400,000 of public money. Funds for widows and orphans, and for some reason he was the only one in charge, so that at the end he hadn't been audited for some eight years. I can just see the long faces they're all wearing now and how they're remembering him! A delightful thought, don't you agree? I'd been marvelling for a whole year now how this seventy-year-old geezer, who suffered from gout and rheumatism, managed to conserve so much energy for debauchery, and – and now we have the answer! It was the widows and orphans – the thought of them alone must have fired him up! . . . I had known about it for a long time, and I was the only one to know, Charpentier told me, and as soon as I found out, I immediately hit him up in a friendly way during Holy Week: "Give me 25,000, or there'll be an audit tomorrow"; and just imagine, he could only come up with 13,000, so it seems that his dying now was very expedient. *Grand-père, grand-père*, do you hear me?'

'*Chèr* Klinevich, I quite agree with you, and there is no need for you . . . to go into such details. Life has so much suffering and torments and so little reward . . . In the end

I wished finally to have some peace and, so far as I see, I hope to glean all I can from here as well . . .'

'I'll wager that he's already sniffed out Katish Berestova!'

'Who? . . . Which Katish is that?' the old man's voice began to tremble with lust.

'Ah-ah, which Katish? The one right here, to the left, five paces from me, ten from you. It's already her fifth day here, and if you knew, *grand-père*, what a little rascal she is . . . from a good family, well brought up and – a monster, an utter monster! I didn't show her to anybody there, I was the only one who knew . . . Katish, answer me!'

'He-he-he!' answered in reply the cracked sound of a girl's voice, in which, however, one could hear something like the jab of a needle. 'He-he-he!'

'A *little blonde girl*?' *Grand-père* babbled haltingly, drawing out the three words.

'He-he-he!'

'I . . . I have long,' babbled the old man, panting, 'dreamed of a little blonde girl . . . about fifteen years old . . . and precisely in circumstances like these . . .'

'Ugh, you monster!' Avdotya Ignatyevna exclaimed.

'Enough!' Klinevich had made up his mind. 'I see that there's excellent material. We'll quickly arrange things for the better here. The main thing is to spend the remaining time enjoyably; but how much time? Hey, you, the government official, did I hear that your name was Lebezyatnikov?'

'Lebezyatnikov, court councillor, Semyon Yevseyich, at your service, and I'm very, very, very glad to make your acquaintance.'

'I don't give a damn whether you're pleased; it's just that it seems you know everything here. Tell me, first of all (I've been wondering about this since yesterday), how is it that we can talk here? After all, we're dead, and yet we can talk; and it seems that we can move as well, and yet we don't talk and we don't move. What's the secret?'

'If you wish, Baron, Platon Nikolayevich could explain this to you better than I.'

'Who's Platon Nikolayevich? Don't shilly-shally, get to the point.'

'Platon Nikolayevich is our local, homespun philosopher, scientist and master of arts. He's put out several little books on philosophy, but for the past three months now he keeps falling sound asleep, so much so that it's impossible to stir him. Once a week he mutters a few words beside the point.'

'Get to the point, get to the point! . . .'

'He explains it all by the simplest fact, namely, that up above, when we were still alive, we mistakenly deemed death there was death. The body comes to life here again, as it were, the residue of life is concentrated, but only in the consciousness. I don't know how to say it – it's as if life continues by inertia. Everything is concentrated, in his opinion, somewhere in the consciousness and continues for another two or three months . . . sometimes even half a year . . . There's one fellow here, for example, who has almost completely decomposed, but once every six weeks he'll still suddenly mutter a word, meaningless, of course, about some *bobok*: "*Bobok, bobok*." But that means that an inconspicuous spark of life still glimmers inside him as well . . .'

'Rather stupid. But then how is it that I smell a stench if I don't have a sense of smell?'

'That's . . . he-he . . . Well, that's where our philosopher gets a bit hazy. It was precisely in regard to the sense of smell that he observed that the stench that is smelled, so to speak, is a moral stench! He-he! The stench coming from our soul, as it were, so that in these two or three months one has time to look back . . . and that this is, so to speak, the final mercy . . . Only it seems to me, Baron, that this is all mystical gibberish, which is quite excusable given his circumstances . . .'

'Enough, and the rest of it, I'm sure, is all nonsense. The main thing is that there's two or three months of life and in the end – *bobok*. I propose that we all spend these two months as pleasantly as possible and to that end we should all arrange things on a different footing. Ladies and gentlemen! I propose that we not be ashamed of anything!'

'Ah, yes, let's, let's not be ashamed of anything!' many voices were heard to say, and, strangely enough, even altogether new voices were heard, which means that meanwhile some others had only just awakened. The bass voice of an engineer, now fully awake, thundered his assent with particular readiness. The girl Katish giggled with delight.

'Ah, how I want not to be ashamed of anything!' Avdotya Ignatyevna exclaimed with rapture.

'Listen, now if even Avdotya Ignatyevna wants not to be ashamed of anything . . .'

'No-no-no, Klinevich, I was ashamed, all the same I was ashamed there, but here I so terribly, terribly wish not to be ashamed of anything!'

'I understand, Klinevich,' the engineer bellowed, 'that you're proposing to arrange life here, so to speak, on a new and rational footing.'

'Well, I don't give a damn about that! As far as that's concerned, let's wait for Kuderyarov, who was brought here yesterday. He'll wake up and explain everything to you. He's such a figure, such a gigantic figure! Tomorrow, I believe, they're bringing another scientist and probably another officer, and, if I'm not mistaken in three or four days a certain feuilletonist and, I believe, his editor as well. However, to hell with them, we'll have our own little group and everything will fall into place on its own. But meanwhile I don't want there to be any lying. That's all I want, because that's the main thing. On earth it's impossible to live and not to lie, for life and lying are synonymous; well, but here for the fun of it we won't lie. The devil take it, the grave does mean something after all! We'll all tell our stories out loud and we won't be ashamed of anything

109

now. I'll tell about myself first. I'm a voluptuary, you know. Up there all this was bound together with rotten ropes. Down with ropes, and let's live these two months in the most shameless truth! Let's strip ourselves bare and be naked!'

'Let's be naked, naked!' the voices all cried out.

'I so terribly, terribly want to be naked!' Avdotya Ignatyevna squealed.

'Ah . . . ah . . . Ah, I see that we're going to have a good time here; I don't want to go see Ecke!'

'No, I would have lived a bit longer, you know, I would have lived a bit longer!'

'He-he-he!' Katish giggled.

'The main thing is that nobody can stand in our way, and even though Pervoyedov, I see, is angry, all the same he can't touch me. *Grand-père*, do you agree?'

'I absolutely, absolutely agree and with the greatest pleasure, provided only that Katish begins with her biography first.'

'I protest, I protest with all my might,' General Pervoyedov pronounced firmly.

'Your Excellency!' the scoundrel Lebezyatnikov prattled and urged in hurried excitement, with his voice lowered, 'Your Excellency, it will be to our advantage to agree. You see, there's this girl . . . and, finally, all these various little things . . .'

'To be sure, there's the girl, but . . .'

'To our advantage, Your Excellency, it would really

and truly be to our advantage! Well, if only as an experiment, well, let's at least give it a try . . .'

'Even in the grave they won't let me rest in peace!'

'First of all, General, you're playing preference in the grave, and secondly, *we don't give a damn about you*,' Klinevich declaimed, emphasizing each word.

'My dear sir, I beg you all the same not to forget yourself.'

'What? But you can't touch me, while I can tease you from here, like Yulka's lapdog. And, first of all, gentlemen, what sort of general is he here? It's there he was a general, but here he's a mere nothing!'

'No, not a mere nothing . . . Here, too, I'm a . . .'

'Here you'll rot in your coffin, and the only thing left of you will be your six brass buttons.'

'Bravo, Klinevich, ha-ha-ha!' the voices roared.

'I served my sovereign . . . I have a sword . . .'

'The only thing your sword's good for is spearing mice; besides, you never drew it.'

'All the same, sir; I comprised a part of the whole.'

'There are all sorts of parts in the whole.'

'Bravo, Klinevich, bravo, ha-ha-ha!'

'I don't understand what exactly a sword is,' the engineer exclaimed.

'We'll run from the Prussians like mice, they'll tear us to pieces,' cried a distant and unfamiliar voice, but one literally transported with delight.

'A sword, sir, is honour!' the general cried, but only I heard him. A prolonged and frenzied roar, melee and clamour broke out, and only Avdotya Ignatyevna's impatient squeals, which bordered on the hysterical, could be heard.

'But quickly, quickly! Ah, when are we going to start being ashamed of nothing!'

'Oh-ho-ho! Truly, my soul is passing through the torments!' resounded the voice of the man of the common people, and . . .

And that's when I suddenly sneezed. It happened without warning and unintentionally, but the effect was startling: everything fell as silent as the grave, and it all vanished like a dream. A truly sepulchral silence ensued. I don't think that they had become ashamed on my account: after all, they'd resolved not to be ashamed of anything! I waited for about five minutes and – not a word, not a sound. Nor can one suppose that they feared that I would inform on them to the police; for what could the police do here? I can only conclude that they must after all have some secret, unknown to us mortals, which they carefully conceal from every mortal.

'Well, my dears,' I thought, 'I'll come visit you again', and with that I left the cemetery.

No, this I will not tolerate; no, indeed, no! It's not *bobok* that troubles me (so that's what this *bobok* turned out to be!).

Depravity in such a place, the depravity of the final hopes, the depravity of flabby and rotting corpses and – not sparing even the final moments of consciousness! They were granted, they were made a present of these moments and . . . But most of all, most of all – in such a place! No, this I will not tolerate . . .

I'll spend some time in other classes of graves here, I'll listen everywhere. That's just what needs to be done, to listen everywhere and not just in one part, in order to come to an understanding. Perhaps I'll stumble on to something comforting.

But I'll definitely go back to them. They promised their biographies and various stories. Ugh! But I'll go, I'll definitely go; it's a matter of conscience!

I'll take it to the *Citizen*; a portrait of one of the editors there was also put in the exhibit. Perhaps he'll publish it.

1873